A Homicidal Publisher's Tale

Books by Linda Mann

The Tavistock Mystery Series

Mist

The Tidemaster

The Corsican Trap

Anyone here seen Kelly?

The Mr Boots Series

Mr Boots

Others

The Chronicles of Edwin Snipe

A Homicidal Publisher's Tale

A Homicidal Publisher's Tale

LINDA MANN

Priory Press

Published by Priory Press Ltd
The Priory, Abbots Way, Abbotswood,
Ballasalla, Isle of Man IM9 3EQ
www.priory-press.co.uk

First published 2014

ISBN 978 0 9574914 7 2

Edited and typeset by
Frances Hackeson Freelance Publishing Services,
Brinscall, Lancs
Printed in Great Britain by
Bell and Bain Ltd, Glasgow

The present day

Light, warm and bright, shines on the scattered papers and I sit back and allow my tired neck a little respite. Somewhere in the distance a vacuum cleaner whines and sucks its way up a blind corridor and is accompanied by a tuneless whistle. Here in my small and tidy room I finally have had the time to finish *The Great Novel* uninterrupted by the usual day-to-day delights of running around after others, fixing meals, cleaning, shopping.

I sit back and for a brief and fleeting moment feel something akin to happiness.

I can hear footsteps approaching; two sets, one a sharp staccato of metal-tipped pointed heels and the other slower, flatter, stealthier and probably rubber-soled.

They stop outside my door and pause. I can almost imagine a whispered conversation and then the door is opened. I cannot turn, cannot even breathe. I glance around at my books and papers, my pens and hastily scribbled notes.

'Alex.'

I stay silently turned from them, wanting to know and not wanting in the same instant.

'The appeal was ... '

I glance again at the finished manuscript, a wonderful hotchpotch of characters, more bodies than Midsomer and a sleuth to rival Miss Marple and John Rebus, and of course completely fictional.

' ... upheld ... Alex you're free!'

'Free?'

'You can go.'

I look again at my tidy desk, lacking the usual paraphernalia of accounts, begging letters from the bank, demands from impoverished writers and that awful howling beast ... the telephone. There have been regular meals at regular times, a library stocked with books and enough material to keep a researcher happy for years and I have had wonderful blessed quiet. Prison has been far better than any holiday and I haven't had to pay a penny.

'Er ... do I have to?' I ask.

One

My name is Alex and I used to live in a small and terribly nice village which nestles in the bowl made by five surrounding hills. By nice I mean pretty; pretty village green, pretty shops, pretty school, pretty houses, there is even a tasteful duck pond and – hidden by trees – a large and baronial manor house. The people, on the other hand, are anything but nice, as they are just people, with all the usual warts and hang-ups that accompany real, non-celebrity, lives.

My house stands to the side of the duck pond, in a slightly elevated position and has been a noose around my neck ever since I took out my first mortgage on the wretched edifice. I live in it and also work from it as a very small and inconspicuous publisher, struggling to borrow from Peter without the bank finding out before I pay Paul. One day I will come across the perfect manuscript, the golden goose that will lay the golden Rowling eggs, the bestseller, the critically acclaimed and widely read literary gem – one day.

Until then I struggle with marketing the books I do have and in keeping my editor and stable of writers reasonably happy. This happiness is usually, for the average writer, the simple sight of their next printed tome and for Caroline my editor, project manager and best friend, a cheque for services rendered which hasn't been post-dated.

I doggedly carried on with my dozen or so titles a year and would have done so up and until retirement or death, if it hadn't have been for that one, nasty, badly written manuscript. The one that turned up in the post completely unsolicited, the one that set out in great detail the true meaning of my favourite word ...

Murder.

A warm and humid afternoon in July three years ago ...

Reasons to kill – pat 1

I sighed and took a sip of lukewarm coffee.

The idiot couldn't even spell 'part'.

Good start to a manuscript that, the first spelling mistake is the fourth word on the first line ... and no I don't count dashes as words ... have they no idea how much the average editor costs?

Still the title is intriguing, *Five Ways to Kill*. I look up, staring, and take another sip of coffee, my brain haring off at a tangent. Five ways, hmmm ... I used to live at a place called Five Ways, bugger to get the car out in the morning.

Might as well read on; it's that or reconcile the bank statements and frankly I just don't have that much gin in the house.

1. Accidentally ...

Er ... how the hell do you kill someone by accident? Ooops, sorry, just happened to smash your head open with a stuffed eel skin, didn't know you had a really thin skull ... won't happen again.

Oh that's what he meant.

I presume it's a he, as he's just sent it in with the initials ATP on the top next to the little c for copyright and a date going back a few years. I suppose that it might be a she, although most women writers do at least use a surname and their spelling is generally speaking much, much better.

Good grief, for God's sake there is no need to do that to a verb and has he no idea about what a comma is? They're being thrown around like confetti at a wedding. I guess the twit thinks that at some point he might actually put one in the right place, eventually, law of probability and all that.

Makes a kind of sense I suppose.

I admit, that the first time I killed, it was a complete accident, a stupid row, when, pissed, as a newt, about a woman, of all things …

Charming!

I couldn't', understand, why he still insisted, on the farce, of her being other than an out and out tart, a prostitute, who had hit the jackpot, he said she was a dancer, some men will beleive anything and he always, did think with his knob, so I hit him tried to nock some sense into him.

Ye gods, he's discovered the full stop!

Only he didn't get up he'd hit his head on a rock and lay very still his eyes wide open and staring but there was nothing behind them nothing aty all I panicked then and rolled him into the water. I stuffed his clothing with rocks as many as \I could find and then I rolled him further out their where weeds and thingsand they began to cover him up. with any luck no one would find him and if they did id be miles away I admit that I took a little souvenir I have no idea why but at the time it seemed to the right thing to do.

And now he's forgotten about the comma. Can I carry on reading this without a hot beverage of some kind? Mustn't have caffeine in it as I'm already floating on the stuff and it's not even elevenses.

Wonder if I have any peppermint tea bags left?

I have and I make a nice cup of tea, open a pack of Garibaldis and go back to my cluttered desk and murder number two or another reason to kill. Not sure I understand the distinction the author is trying to make.

2. For money ...

Well okay, assassins kill for cash ... wonder if I could get a discount for a bulk order?

I look at the bank statements nestling in a heap next to the cheque and paying-in books and ruminate upon all those that could do with a bullet in the brain: the bank manager, the bloke in head office, the director of the bank, the chap who took me down to that little room in the basement and chopped my card in half whilst telling me that it was for my own good ... shifty-eyed little bastard. I take a sip of tea and a bite out of a biscuit and continue reading.

I was partly right, he was referring to soldiers, although to my mind not in a nice way and for several pages. The tit could rant for England and the press would have a field day with page three ... and possibly four, five and six.

3. In anger ...

Really?

Now isn't that a surprise, only wouldn't that be under accident?

Apparently not and then he goes on, at some considerable length, about the psychology of the average murder. There are a bunch of statistics and an impressive-looking graph and pie chart.

Oh God he's coloured it in ... If he thinks I'm paying that shower in Shropshire extra for coloured illustrations he's got another think coming. I need another biscuit.

4. Deliberately ...

Oh good, now I know where we are, after all you can't publish crime without a body or two. I mean what would be the point?

More bloody pie charts.

This is getting to be a bit worthy.

I really can't see old Mrs Coaltit from the post office reading this in her back room. She's a great reader, head always in a book even when you have only minutes to catch the post and don't have a stamp. Never knew a woman read quite so much and so often, must have something to do with shagging the awful Albert. They must be sixty if they're a day, it's almost disgusting. And when Mrs Albert finds out ...

Aargh – we are back to point four again.

Can't wait to see what he has for number five, as I personally, off the top of my head, can't think of one.

5. Because you like it ...

In red – the tit now has coloured *headings* ... coloured. Now I really need a drink. How can anyone *like* the act of murder? Oh my God, not another bloody pie chart.

No, *three* of the buggers.

I'm beginning to lose the will to live, let alone read any further.

I shall send it back with a compliments slip and a handwritten note to the effect that we only accept fiction.

I shall of course wish him well with his next publisher, after all you never know he might find someone else willing to expend time on teaching him the rudiments of grammar and it could be the next big thing. No point in upsetting the pillock.

Why first time authors never do their homework and find out what publisher does what and with whom, I have no idea.

I mean to say, even if they can't afford the *Writers and Artists Yearbook* the library always has a copy somewhere. Unless the librarian is using the damn thing.

Anyway, not my problem.

My problem is waiting down the road at the Pink Panther Café for my thoughts on his latest and least likeable literary offering. The fact that only a handful of people won't feel offended by his obvious descent into the gutter, has by and large failed to hit his over-inflated ego. I have absolutely no idea why the hell they had to award him that wretched prize, as he's gone from perfectly readable if a little crude, to literary obtrusiveness and downright smut in only a matter of months.

There is absolutely no way that I want to publish any of it, apart from possibly the title which is frankly the only bit that isn't lewd and doesn't include any swears starting with 'f', 'b' or indeed 'c'.

To be honest, what with one thing and another, I'm not really sure if I'll have a company to publish with by the end of the month.

* * *

'Look Marcus, I'm sure that it will have a ready market somewhere but it just isn't with me.'

A perfectly polite refusal and frankly one which any other writer would have accepted, albeit grudgingly. We would then have finished our adequate and rather sloppy lasagnes and gone our separate ways. What should not have happened was what did and in front of the entire village.

I don't think I have ever been so insulted in my life, well certainly not sober.

Talk about biting the hand that feeds.

Jasmine Smurfitt was serving us, a very nice young lady. Just because she wears a lot of black and has her nose pierced there was no need for Marcus to shout at her about bloodsuckers and coffins. Jasmine looked like she was going to cry and then the chef actually lumbered out of his kitchen and asked us to leave.

It was so embarrassing.

Everyone knows that Marcus is my golden goose; in fact he's one of the few really profitable scribes that I have. This will not go down well with the bank, represented in person by the truly terrifying Trudy. I'm sure that she must have, at some point, have passed some kind of exam; I'm just not convinced that it could have been in either banking, economics or customer service.

Marcus let rip on the way out of the café, in a wordy and unintelligible diatribe. In fact I can't remember quite how much drivel he spouted but enough to alienate everyone having a peaceful lunch. He even offended our local law enforcer, which will mean that I'm going to be on the receiving end of PC Duncan Macleod's wrath for the next week or so. I'm not even going to be able to leave the wheelie bin outside without acquiring a parking ticket, until at least Christmas.

I tried to placate the crowd, now baying for blood, before paying the bill and stomping off after him down the high street and towards the local railway station. I could feel the eyes following me as I tried to catch up with the rabid fool. I really did try to calm him down, to pour oil on troubled waters.

I even made a few very small suggestions in order that I could at least print part of his epic opus. You know what he did?

He pulled my lapels, actually stood at the side of the platform and lifted me up by my lapels. Buttons flying left, right and centre.

He was actually quite, quite mad.

Not just mad, bad and dangerous to know; that sort of Byronic bluster is all part and parcel of the writing world. No, dear old Marcus had completely and utterly lost the plot. Thrown the proverbial baby out with the proverbial bathwater and gone critical.

So there we were eyeball to eyeball, him with spittle punctuating every foul word, and me with my heels several inches from the ground.

Nobody was on either platform, not even young Brian who waters the plants and feeds the chicken. Medium old Brian, the ticket collector-cum-station master, was presumably still in the Pink Panther feeling insulted, and the only living thing within earshot, apart from us, was the station cat, a rancid-looking creature of the black and white variety, with only one ear and a tail with a ninety-degree kink in the middle.

I honestly thought that Marcus had finally been cutting his medication with heroin or vice versa, or even adding the odd cleaning product. So I pushed him.

I pushed him very hard in the stomach. And as he released me I pushed him again.

What neither of us had taken into account was that although his train back to the smoke was going to be another half hour at least, the City express was actually early.

There was an awful moment when time truly did stand still, as he overbalanced sideways and fell. The roar of the train rushing past, the wind which almost sucked me after it and then nothing but the platform on the other side and the cat, watching me with unblinking yellow eyes.

Marcus had gone.

Trembling with fright I looked over the side of the platform, expecting at the very least, some sort of mangled body part, but there was nothing.

Not a single solitary drop of anything.

I felt my heart thumping, racing and the next I knew I was sitting on a bench in the sun with my head between my knees and I was blubbing for England, Scotland and Wales.

Young Brian found me.

By then I had stopped watering the planters and had pulled myself together. He asked me how I was and I must have replied, because he nodded and then wandered off clutching a pair of rusting secateurs, to do something horrible to the baskets of gaily fluttering petunias. The World Cup had been mentioned at some point, because apparently the station cat could play better. The cat continued to watch me with steady interested eyes and after a while I looked at my watch, realised that an hour had passed, including

Marcus's intended transportation, and not knowing what else to do, I went home.

* * *

I watched every news programme I could get on my elderly television and was the first one down at the newsagents the following morning. This was in itself nothing unusual, as I'm normally glued to the step when a book is due out. I used to be there praying to any God that might be listening to give me a wonderful paragraph or two of complimentary praise. Now I'd quite happily settle for a single line of anything. Even vitriol could be controversial enough to get someone to read the thing.

And let's face it, the general public don't have to like the book; they don't even have to read it, as far as I'm concerned the important thing is that they buy it.

Eventually, I bought a few of the more lurid tabloids, just in case they'd found out about Marcus first and also the local rag and its cousin from across the border.

I lumbered back home clutching them to my bosom and didn't actually feel like breathing properly until I'd closed the door on the world and the papers were glaring up at me from the kitchen table. Realising that I hadn't actually eaten since the previous lunchtime, I threw a couple of eggs in a bowl with black pepper and cream, thrust bread in the toaster, the type that tastes like cardboard but comes packed with extra vitamins and essential minerals, and put the kettle on to boil.

There was nothing in the local rag or its stablemate. Perhaps it was too soon for our local hacks?

I scrambled the eggs, buttered the toast and made a pot of tea before lugging the whole lot into the lounge. I sat staring at my breakfast and then had to get up and retrieve the rest of the papers.

I perused each and every one and discovered nothing of significant interest, apart from the fact that young Brian was probably right about the cat and Victoria Beckham was thinking of having another tattoo. The poor woman can't have any skin left, I thought, as I absentmindedly squirted ketchup on my egg. It was a mistake.

Suddenly not as hungry as I had been, I turned to the local paper again, just in case I had missed something.

I hadn't.

My mug of tea, which sat cooling gently beside the congealing egg and saturated fats, wobbled violently as my mobile phone vibrated urgently beside it.

Tentatively I answered the thing.

It was Terrible Trudy from the bank requesting my presence. I knew I should have reconciled those stupid statements. Too late now.

Promising to see her on Friday, I hung up and surveyed the wreckage of my breakfast and the piles of abused newsprint. There wasn't a single solitary line about Marcus. It was just as if he had vanished from the face of the earth the moment I had pushed him into the arms of that wretched train.

To hell with this, I thought, and then the doorbell rang.

I lumbered from the lounge, crossed the hall and flung it open, nearly causing another accident as our friendly constable staggered backwards. Luckily he found the handrail in time and glaring at me from under his helmet, he completed whatever he was writing in the notebook he was clutching, tore a page out, handed it to me with an evil snort and the words, 'For the bin' and waddled back down the steps to the road beyond.

I closed the door upon his departing blue-clad backside and leant against it, heart pounding erratically and breath coming in huge bursts. I swallowed and the horrid prickles of adrenalin coursing up and down my arms and legs worsened as the panic attack settled in for the duration.

'*Sod the tea*!' I said aloud and then I raced off, found my emergency litre bottle of gin, opened it and poured a very large nip into a very small glass.

Two

It's been five days since I pushed Marcus under the 2.30 City express and still nothing has turned up in the press, under a train or anywhere. In fact I'm beginning to wonder if I actually did do it.

What if Marcus didn't die?

What if, by some miracle, he managed to cling on and crawl through an open window? James Bond, even the naff blond one, manages it. Marcus of the thinning oily hairline, pale writer's skin, flaccid paunch and thin stick-like limbs was not the sort of chap you could imagine delivering chocolate by helicopter at the dead of night, or for that matter at any time, certainly not in daylight.

What if he's just waiting and he's going to come back and take his revenge ... what if he wants to blackmail me into publishing his awful, horrid, nasty, little book?

What the hell am I going to do?

I know – I'll report him as a missing person, then he can't say that I never told anyone, just that I forgot to do it immediately.

It's been five days: even I don't have senior moments that last that long.

Perhaps he'll be nice about it. Hmm, perhaps the Pope likes homosexuals and Tony Blair wasn't a shit.

I was still talking to the damp patch on the ceiling when my mobile rang. I didn't recognise the caller ID, so picked it up much in the manner of an unexploded bomb.

It's mother, demanding to know if I'm eating.

After I discussed my eating habits, had been castigated about the number of swears in the last book and the fact that tantric sex ought to be illegal, she then wittered on at great length about the fact that I didn't have a partner and she doesn't have any grandchildren. In the end I cut her off in her prime as the landline rang and rang.

It wasn't, after a heart-stopping moment, Marcus either. It was my editor demanding to know if I'd seen the news.

'What news?' I spluttered.

'The increase in paper costs!' She shouted at me as if I was some child with hearing difficulties. I put the phone down on her as well.

Paper was the least of my problems.

The phone rang again and I answered it with something like a squawk.

Nobody said anything but I could hear whoever it was listening.

I dropped it like a very hot, hot thing. My head pounded and my mouth was dry. I tried to remember if anyone could possibly have known what I may or may not have done. When I eventually got up the courage to listen to the breathing again, it had gone and the phone was dead.

He's coming to get me, I know he is.

I will have to publish his book, it will sell three copies and I will go into administration.

I'm doomed.

I think about going out, and pick up the car keys, then stop – what if he's waiting outside for me? What if he's actually in the car, on the back seat, under a blanket, clutching an axe or a long length of cheese wire? What if he sticks a bag over my head and gaffer-tapes me to the steering wheel? What if I just stay inside until I die?

He could get into the house, he knows where I live. Not difficult when you run a company from the dining room. At the time it really saved on the overheads, now I'm not so sure it was worth it.

What do I do? What *do* I do?

After all it was just a bloody accident.

Three

It is now six days since I pushed my one and only best-selling author under a train and they still haven't found the body. This means that he could have survived and now he is coming to get me, which is why I've decamped to the potting shed on my allotment.

He doesn't know I have one – potting shed or allotment – so I should, in theory, be all right for a bit. It's quite comfortable really and daffodil bulbs are almost edible if you don't chew.

There was a knock on the door, tentative I admit, more of a scrabble than a knock.

'Who is it?' I whispered through a knot in the wood, as I searched for some sort of weapon.

'It's only me, dear.'

Oh God, it's mother. I closed my eyes and took a deep, deep, breath.

'What are you doing in there?'

'Looking for a spade.'

'Oh.'

I opened the door a tad; I was clutching a bag of compost and a small trowel.

My mother looked at me and then glanced behind her. There were two figures standing in her shadow and one was a policeman.

'Are you going to be long in there?' she finally asked.

'No, I've finished,' I replied whilst feverishly looking for a rope or anything that I could turn into a noose. The only thing I could see was some aged bean string and I wasn't sure that it could hold my traditionally proportioned body.

'Good, because these gentlemen say that they would like a word.'

Only my mother would call the local constabulary gentlemen and mean it. Our local constable shuffled uncomfortably – as well he should for giving me a ticket stating that my wheelie bin was parked in a reckless fashion and that it was a danger to pedestrians. It was halfway up the drive, at the side of the oil tank and the plonker didn't give that a ticket!

'Alex, put that trowel down now and go home, you're absolutely filthy. But you can bring that bag of compost because the pot by the front door needs re-planting.'

I shut my eyes. Perhaps if I stay like this they will all go away and I can have a perfectly good nervous breakdown in peace and quiet, I thought.

'Alex are you listening to me?'

I opened my eyes.

Nope they were all still there. So I smiled at them, which appeared to worry everyone, although why I wasn't sure. Then I went home and caught sight of myself in the hall mirror and let out a short shriek. I looked like the spitting image version of Margaret Thatcher on speed. I raced up the stairs to the bathroom, had a shower, changed into clothes without creases in them, brushed my teeth making sure that I flossed properly and eventually went down to the lounge, where the policemen were still waiting. My mother staggered in from the kitchen with a tea trolley I didn't know that I even had. It was weighed down with a cafetiere of coffee, a pot of tea and a jug of hot chocolate. There were sandwiches with the crusts cut off, scones neatly halved and lathered in cream and pink stuff and a huge, great big iced sponge with cherries on the top.

I sat and had a napkin promptly tucked under my chin. I could see out of the corner of my eye that the representatives of the law were all ready to snigger, right up to the point when she tucked a napkin under their chins as well.

We attempted to drink our hot beverages, whilst discussing the weather, the fact that America has a black person in charge and doesn't he look like Mr Jones who used to own the greengrocers next door to that nice man who murdered his wife. I choked on my scone and was sternly admonished for spluttering on the carpet.

At that point the doorbell rang and mother demanded that I go and answer it, which I did, as even Marcus clutching a lethal weapon was the better alternative to one of my mother's teas. Especially as the red stuff on the scone turned out to be tomato ketchup and one of the sandwiches had egg mayonnaise, sardine and banana in it. I dreaded to think what the cake was made from, as I knew damn well that I didn't have any cherries in the house.

I thrust the door open and gasped. There was a large man who looked a bit like Vinnie Jones wearing a white coat.

'She's in there,' I croaked.

He marched past me and gently but firmly removed the cake knife from my mother's hands, steered her well away from the rest of the cutlery and manhandled her down the hall, out of the front door and into the waiting van. It had *'Happy Oaks Residential Care home'* emblazoned on the side in black copperplate script.

My visitors exchanged mutually relieved looks and then asked simultaneously where the bathroom was.

I pointed them in the direction of the one under the stairs and the one next to my guest bedroom and they departed, very quickly, to the safety of the nearest toilet bowl.

I fleetingly wondered if I had time to raid the change jar and escape with the car pointed firmly towards the M8 and the Outer Hebrides.

Instead I wheeled the trolley into the kitchen and made a proper pot of tea, without using Bovril or any Lea and Perrins.

Finally my guests returned, looking slightly less green and I proffered steaming cups of pukka tea. They sipped in silence and then one of them extracted a notebook from his pocket, whilst the other one asked quite nicely when was the last time I saw Marcus Foolstop.

'Marcus?' I said, playing for time.

They both looked at me in a blank fashion and I swallowed. Then I remembered that PC Duncan Macleod, the one in uniform, was actually in the Pink Panther Café when Marcus verbally exploded. I took a deep breath and tried to keep my breathing even. This was no time for one of my panics.

'It must have been a good week ago.'

'And how was he?' asked the chap in a suit who my mother had forgotten to introduce.

'Angry. We had a row about his latest book.'

'Why?'

'He thought that it was the best thing he'd ever done and I thought it was crap.'

'Bad, was it?'

I looked at PC Macleod and remembered that there was a reason why his nickname was McPlod.

'With the proverbial knobs on,' I replied. 'Anyway you must have heard him, it was in the Pink Panther Cafe last week, he called you ... '

'*That* was Marcus Foolstop?'

'Yes.'

'Oh.'

They exchanged another one of their shared looks and I wondered if they should just get a room.

'Why?'

Please, please get on with it, I shouted in my head, a silent scream of fear edging its way from my brain to my vocal chords.

'When did you see him last?'

Here it was then, the million dollar, go straight to jail, do not pass Go or collect two hundred pounds, question.

'At the railway station.'

'The one in Little Comfrey?'

'Yes. The railway station. The one here, in the village.'

They exchanged another look.

'Not the one at Lower Barton?'

Lower Barton? Just how much of my mother's version of coffee had they drunk? I didn't even have to fake the confused look as by then it was totally effortless.

'No that's miles away ... I just walked him to the station before anyone else was insulted, not that there was anyone left in the village to insult, and left him on the platform.'

Well, strictly speaking I did leave him on the platform, so it wasn't a direct lie, after all I had been brought up not to lie to the police. It was like wetting the bed and being rude to the vicar, it could get you into terrible trouble, to say nothing of having your backside tanned with a slipper and being grounded for a week.

I was, I had to admit, more than a bit puzzled as Lower Barton is a few miles away, at the side of the River Gaunt, which runs just beyond the parish boundary.

'Look, can't you tell me what this is all about?'

'The thing is, we may have found the body of Marcus Foolstop.'

'You *may* have?'

'Too soon to tell for certain at this stage, it's just that ... '

'What?'

'We can't find anyone who can identify him and as you were the last to see him ... '

'I'll get my coat.' I sighed and toddled off.

So that's how I got to stand an hour or so later in the local morgue looking at the white and fully clothed remains of my erstwhile and very, very, dead writer and one-time friend, Marcus Foolstop.

The only thing that I found a trifle puzzling was that his suit was absolutely sodden.

That and the fact that he didn't look even a bit squished.

'Oh yes, that's Marcus,' I stuttered, before keeling over and fainting on the floor.

* * *

I came to, only to find that they were still there and so was Marcus.

I was, I have to admit, rather relieved about the whole thing. So much so, that when they asked if they could have a quiet word, I was more than happy to help them in their enquiries. I got to sit in a room which had windows you could see out of and furniture which didn't look like it had been nailed to the floor, so I presumed that somehow I wasn't a suspect and was really helping.

Coffee was produced and a plate of biscuits and then the inquisition started.

'Was Mr Foolstop worried about anything?'

'Um ... well ... I wasn't going to publish his latest book. That sort of upset him, although the anger was probably the thing I noticed most.'

'So would he have been depressed?'

'Marcus was always depressed, it's what he did between writing, swearing and drinking.'

'Did he take drugs?'

'I don't know ... I mean, I was his publisher not his mother.'

I did try to help, I really did, but every question they threw at me seemed to get even stranger ... they even wanted to read some of his books. Eventually I managed to ask what it was all about and they did finally deign to enlighten me.

Apparently, the body of Marcus Foolstop had been found floating beside a discarded supermarket trolley in the river Gaunt two days previously and they thought he'd died several days before that. They found certain drugs in his system, which didn't appear to surprise anyone and probably contributed to his mood from the moment we had met that day in the Pink Panther. The upshot was that they believed that he had, due to my rejection of his life's work and under the influence of drugs and alcohol, thrown himself from the train as it was crossing over the Gaunt. Someone thought that they saw him on the platform at Lower Barton but they couldn't be sure, because they'd glimpsed him very briefly through the windows of their train when the express went through.

I sat stunned, and then I had a thought; what if Marcus had somehow managed to cling like a limpet to the train? And what if that's what the witness had seen? Marcus wasn't on the platform; he was on the side of the 2.30 train. In fact he was clinging to the side, right up to the point when the train went over the river and then he fell off. Perhaps he let go thinking that the water would break his fall. And I suppose if the tide had been in and there had been more than a foot or so of the wet stuff, it might have.

Poor Marcus, I was almost beginning to feel sorry for the sod. Until I remembered some of the things he'd said about me and also that I wouldn't have to pay him his royalty cheque. Well I'd still pay; it just wouldn't be cashed for a bit. Well, not until they sorted out his affairs and, knowing Marcus and his patented floor filing system, that would take some time.

It was suicide. They all believed he had committed suicide.

It wasn't an accident.

I had actually gotten away with murder.

Four

The crematorium was almost full, and a lot of the ladies were wearing hats. There must have been a good thirty or so collected writers, editors, graphic artists and illustrators, plus a smattering of booksellers and one lowly local journalist, who looked like he had a terrible cold and consequently no one would sit next to him.

I had arranged the vicar, sorted out the Order of Service, bought and arranged the flowers. A tasteful bunch of gladioli and poison ivy, something Marcus had mentioned once in one of his books. I'd even taken the trouble to pick the hymns and had invited everyone who'd had anything to do with his books or the publishing firm I was trying to keep above water. I had hoped for a bit more interest from the press though, especially after one of the Sundays, either the *Observer* or *Mail* had done a piece on his sad demise and likened him to Virginia Woolf. Although I had a feeling that she had filled her pockets full of pebbles and walked into the sea, I suppose it made a kind of sense in that both of them had drowned. Even the *Mail* wasn't daft enough to compare them as writers!

We all stood and watched in an almost companionable silence as the coffin disappeared, the curtains wrapping themselves around it until the final view of one solitary brass-coloured handle. Then there were a few words from the elderly vicar I'd found in the Yellow Pages and we all trooped out of a side door to the raucous beat of 'Spirit in the Sky' by Wizard. I stood beside the vicar and pressed the flesh as all of my invited guests sidled by and then we all went back to my place for drinks and sandwiches. My mother had not had anything to do with the catering, although she was there accompanied by a minder even more frightening than the Vinnie Jones impersonator. I presumed that they would frisk her before she left, as the time before last she had walked off with the television remote and a small egg-whisk.

Caroline cornered me between the prawn vol-au-vents and the turkey sandwiches and after helping herself to two each of the aforementioned comestibles, advised me that on no account was I to even consider publishing the little shit's last work. Her words not mine. Apparently he'd sent her a copy by recorded delivery, as the last time he'd tried the self-same stunt of getting to her first, the dog had eaten it.

'I wasn't going to,' I muttered between a mouthful of chicken satay and a glug of cheap Cava.

'Good! It was utter drivel from start to finish and badly spelt drivel at that,' she muttered before fixing me with a baleful stare. 'And what are we going to do about Leonora's cover?'

We both looked towards the writer in question and sighed in unison.

Leonora Midora is one of my more prolific writers. She used to write for Mills and Boon, until her books became rather too saucy even for them and now she sends her naughty chick lit to me. She's popular, and she sells,which is more important. She's always on the list of required reading at libraries and hospitals and wherever she goes has a very vocal and faithful following. She's also a poisonous, twisted, middle-aged tyrant who makes Lucrezia Borgia look like a lovable and helpless novice nun in comparison. On the surface Leonora comes across as being a wonderful mother, devoted wife and all round paid-up member of the WI, but what she really is would make your hair curl. Unfortunately by the time the so-called newest best friend or associate twigs this, she's got so much on them, usually with pictures, that they will do anything just so that they don't have to put up with her any longer. I can't actually remember which of her ex-husbands informed me that a million was not too much to pay to prise her talons off him, but I think it was the one that went off to breed sheep in the Orkneys. Or it may have been the chap that flew off to Goa to find himself and was never seen or heard from again.

Leonora had also recently fallen out with Shelley, the artist who normally did the images for her covers. These were particularly good and atmospheric, helped the books sell like hot potatoes and more importantly were part of brand Leonora. Shelley was one of the very few graphic artists who could work for the miserable old cow, possibly because they had never actually met. Unfortunately Shelley had come down from whatever Scottish commune she was living in and blithely rang the old bat up. Leonora asked her out to lunch and then tried to get her to pay the bill, simply by going outside to take a phone call and never coming back. Shelley was, as all artists are, absolutely broke and had to tearfully call me from the kitchen where she was up to her elbows in steam and dirty plates. I paid the bill, gave her a cup of tea and put her on the next train back to the wet and woolly wilds of some sea loch on the West coast. Now she won't even be in the same room as Leonora and she certainly won't have anything to do with her covers. Which was a bit unfortunate because we had a book about to come out, that even Caroline reckoned was pretty damn good but we had no cover. More importantly, we had no way of getting one. For weeks I had hunted around for another artist, but they were either bloody good and booked up until next Christmas, totally useless, or – even worse – possibly quite gifted but straight out of art college. Not a bad thing in itself, but it did mean that they had no idea how to put together a brief at very short notice and deliver something we could use that would be eye-catching and at the same time have any bearing on the actual book and our target readership. Leonora had stood upon her dignity, blamed me for all the fuss and now she was talking about finding another publisher.

At any other time I would have put out the celebration bunting but I'd spent quite a lot already on the advertising, the launch itself and the marketing material. I'd even had a cheap job lot of silk flowers made up in China, to give out with the first five hundred books. The entire thing had cost an arm and a leg and on the strength of it I had borrowed quite a bit from the Terrible Trudy, who was hell bent on either extracting an inflated amount of loan interest and the capital back from the firm, or like Shylock, a pound of flesh from me personally. And she wouldn't give the proverbial rat's arse for it not having any blood in it.

'I'll sort something out,' I muttered.

'You'd better,' Caroline hissed back and then marched off to annoy someone else.

I stood and watched her go, then turned and surveyed my assembled guests. It wasn't a bad turnout and at least two extra members of the Fourth Estate had turned up for the free booze. Marcus would have actually been quite proud. Well he would have been in the old days before fame and the onset of his snorting anything white up his nose, or what was left of it.

'So how's it going?'

I goggled: it was the Terrible Trudy, resplendent in a dark purple suit, with a little black fascinator of net and feathers. Crow probably, or possibly an albatross that had fallen on hard times.

'How's what going?'

'Things.'

I smiled a trifle nervously and could feel sweat pooling under the arms of my linen suit. I was in shock. Terrible Trudy was making small talk.

'A friend of mine told me that you are actually a really good publisher, astute and on the side of the writer.'

My mouth formed the 'oh' sound but nothing came out, as I was temporarily struck dumb. Not by the thought of the friend but simply that she had one she didn't have to contact by Ouija board.

'I didn't really know what you did before, well not properly.'

'Oh.' This time I mouthed the word and sound came out.

'It's just that I've written a bit of a book about the murder of a bank manager and wondered if you'd read it. Oh – and don't worry about the cost of all this, I'm sure we can work something out to our mutual benefit.' She smiled, handed me a Fortnum and Mason plastic bag and sauntered off in the awful Leonora's direction. I blinked and then I swallowed and then I emptied the nearest bottle into my glass. It was green but after the shock I'd just had, I really didn't care.

* * *

I had an even bigger shock when I finally took the time to extract Trudy's manuscript from the bag because it was really rather good, but oh my, the thought of actually working with her ...

Five

I was still trying to find an artist for Leonora, the deadline being only days away, as Caroline constantly advised me by email, text and latterly phone call, when I decided to attend a local art gallery's grand fest of local and mainly unknown artists. I once read a brilliant definition by Jeff Lindsay of a certain type of modern art which I will always remember '... a sculpture that looked like a geometry lesson having sex in a hardware *bin* ... ' and yes it was that sort of modern art and that sort of gallery.

It was whilst I was standing looking at something which resembled nothing more nor less than a giant green scrotum that I was accosted by the beaming and rotund figure of Charley Moist, the gallery owner.

'You came,' he leered at me.

'Thought us creative types ought to stick together,' I simpered and batted my eyelashes at him. Good God, I thought, exactly what had they put in the cocktails?

'Too true, so do you like it?' he asked, pointing his pinkie at the dreadful daub in front of us.

'Er ... '

'It's Ode to a Gooseberry.'

'Really? '

'Guess how much it's worth?'

'Um ...'

'Well let me tell you that last week I had it up for five hundred plus the frame.'

I looked again at the dreadful thing; it was truly hideous. 'Um five fifty including delivery?'

He chortled and pinched my left buttock. 'Nope 50,000 smackers and next week it could be worth twice that.'

'What?' I cried – he had to be joking. 'What about the credit crunch, loss of confidence and all that?'

'Thing is, my sweet, that now that the banks aren't safe the clever money ... '

'Being clever?'

'*Exactement*! Clever money ... '

'Your average crime lord?'

'Or celebrity, has started investing in art. Makes sense really, as it doesn't go down in price and they can move it around and no questions asked.'

I looked up at the ugly and unpleasant image above us and frowned.

'What you see is the frame. Take it away, roll it up and it's as good as a bankers draft ... better in fact as no banker was involved in the first place.'

'But why this painting?' I asked. 'Why not that one over there?' I pointed at a glutinous squiggle on canvas, which had then been pebble dashed with something that looked like tapioca pudding.

'Ah well you see, the one over there is by Darrah Daubson and Darrah is helping to serve the drinks and the giant gooseberry is by Raven Devine.'

'And Raven is?' I looked around, hoping to catch a glimpse of this gifted and promising artist.

'No love, you won't find our Raven here, well not in corporeal form. It was very sad really when all's said and done, but young Raven came out of the Bush and Lantern, absolutely smashed out of her skull and fell in front of a bus. Before she died I couldn't give her stuff away ... now she's dead I'm thinking of re-hanging everything she had in that poxy rat-hole of a studio, even the one she did at nursery school that her mum stuck on the fridge as a joke.'

'A joke?'

'Sort of ... don't get too big for your booties.'

'You were better when you were three?'

'Yes.'

He surveyed the appalling thing again.

'Anyway I can see you're quite taken with the Gooseberry, have you seen her Ode to a Banana and Two Cherries?'

I shook my head, whereupon I was steered around the gallery until we ended up at another excruciatingly awful mess of acrylic that didn't look a bit like a banana but did look very much like something else entirely.

'Remind you of anything?'

My bottom was pinched again and then with the words 'Must mingle, how about dinner?' he was off.

A young man with green and lilac hair wafted over clutching a tray of badly stuffed quails' eggs and stood at my side.

'Darrah, isn't it?' I asked, taking one of the stuffed eggs.

'So right,' he mumbled.

'Good, isn't it?' I beamed, pointing to the painting in front of us.

'Bloody dog turd on canvas,' he growled.

'So, not good then?'

'No. But she's dead, so it doesn't really matter does it?' he complained as he wandered away.

It was then that it hit me. Marcus had recently had an increase in book sales – not much, but definitely more sales than before he became lawn feed. What if you had someone die in a more flamboyant fashion, what if ... ?

'Darling! Fancy meeting you here? I didn't think culture was really your thing at all ... lovely outfit that. I always think so, whenever I see you in it. But really it wouldn't hurt to splash out a bit more on your image, rather lets us down you know.'

I smiled sweetly down on Leonora, whilst silently thinking, *Fuck you to pal.* I was about to reply when I had an idea, a really good one and I wanted to go somewhere quiet and think about it. I also wanted to get at my computer and have a look at the sales figures, the before and after ones. So instead of letting rip with a few choice observances on mutton dressed as lamb I grinned, bore it and fled as fast as I could back to the relative safety of the office.

* * *

Charley Moist was right; death did increase sales, in fact with some of my rivals quite markedly but only in certain circumstances and usually controversial ones at that.

I sat back in my chair and stared at the ceiling whilst thoughts chased each other around my brain.

I needed to kill a writer and not just any writer, oh no, one from my own stable and one that would have increased figures if he or she died ... Someone with lots of titles I could reprint and possibly one that we could get straight out there posthumously and one ...

My thoughts tailed off.

Leonora would be an ideal candidate ... and if I played my cards right a very profitable one too.

Besides – who would actually miss her?

Six

It was midnight a day after the 'art' show and I was hiding in a shrub at the bottom of Leonora's garden waiting for her to come back from a debauched night out with her agent. I'd read her last but one book twice and made a few notes to get the first sex scene right; I'd even collected all the things that I wasn't sure that Leonora would have ready to hand. All I had to do was to wait for her taxi to leave the wreckage and it would be 'chocks away', or whatever those air force types she kept banging on about would say.

I waited and checked my watch again. Bits of shrubbery were beginning to dig into bits of me and my nose itched. I then felt something creep stealthily into the folds of my balaclava ... and oh my God it had brought its friends. I was just about to take the damn thing off, when a car drew up. Leonora staggered out, trying to pull something out with her, but whoever it was, hung onto the overhead strap and wouldn't get out. The cab driver erupted grumbling from his side of the cab, lumbered round to her side and extracted her long painted talons from the poor cornered sod's clothing. The cab driver then glared at her from his great height and lumbered back to the driver's side and got in. Then he opened the passenger window about six inches and shouted something at her. Leonora screamed some sort of profanity and then threatened not to pay him.

There was a muttered conversation from inside the cab and the window wound down another six inches. 'Too late lady, the bloke's already paid me,' the cabbie shouted back with a certain amount of glee in his voice. Then he hurtled off, tyres and gears screeching in protest at the high speed getaway.

Leonora screamed in frustration and then promptly vomited into the herbaceous border edging her drive. At that point a light across the road went on in an upper window and a head peeked out. It then saw who was screaming and was very hastily withdrawn, only to be followed by another head which shouted at Leonora to piss off and go to bed, and that was the polite version.

Leonora staggered to her front door and then tried to insert her door key.

The party inside my woolly disguise had by that point decided to eat me, so I foolishly took the thing off, which made the shrubbery wobble.

'Whose tat?' Leonora drunkenly asked.

'Er me,' I replied, standing up straight and advancing towards her.

'You look like my publisher but you can't be her, she's fat and short and middle-aged.'

'Older more adorable younger brother,' I replied hastily. Fat huh? Short huh? I am so going to make her suffer.

'Alex never talks about you.'

'Black sheep of the family,' I answered with a bit of a leer. 'Let me get that for you.' I took the key, careful to only touch it with the gloves I had on and opened the door.

She looked up at me and then down, which was a bit embarrassing, and then she looked back up and grinned.

'And there is nothing wrong with that,' she leered short-sightedly. And then she gave a ghastly girly giggle and almost pushed me over in her haste to get me inside. It was at that point that another light went on and another head poked itself out of another of her immediate neighbour's windows.

'Leonora, for God's sake go to bed!' it shouted.

'What the hell do you think I'm trying to do?' she shouted back. 'I even have a nice young man to assist me.' She smiled at me and the head disappeared from view at the same time as the words 'Poor sod,' wafted our way on the breeze.

The burglar alarm, the one that she had triggered by opening the door, was now at full wail and exasperatedly she began to punch every button on the pad, totally forgetting that she had one of those plastic tags and that all she had to do was to wave it in front of the sensor. I held my breath but miraculously she finally remembered that it was on her key ring, thrust it in front of the little red sensor and the heinous noise suddenly stopped.

'Just going to powder my nose,' she snorted, breathing heavy fumes of garlic, wine and vomit in my direction before turning away. In a split second I extracted the leather cosh from the front of my trousers and smacked her with it. I actually hit her as hard as I could on the side of her head. She half-turned and then folded up in front of me.

I had, I reckoned, either just a few minutes before she would regain consciousness or several hours. It was hard to tell but as she was still breathing she couldn't have had an eggshell-thin skull. I then hauled her up to the bathroom and started to run the bath. Next, while the bath was filling, I divested her of her vomit splattered clothes and half-pushed, half-pulled her into the water, which slopped over the side. The water must have been a bit on the cold side, because at that point she woke up and began to struggle; that was until she realised that she was naked. She then spotted the candles that I had carefully laid around the bath, the crucifix hanging from the door, the red rose petals on the floor and the copy of her book in my hand. She gave me a huge and far too familiar grin and licked her lips.

'Oh you naughty, naughty, bad boy!' she cooed. 'All you had to do was to ask.' And then she held out her hands in front of her.

I guess that by then she had remembered just what she had put in on pages thirty-six to seven of her last published book *Tied up with Roses.*

I looped the silk scarf around her hands, tied her feet spread-eagled to the bath taps and thrust the large marble dildo inside her. Well it looked very much like marble and it was heavy enough to be marble except I had bought it from Ann Summers for £9.99 batteries not included, so it can't have been.

By that point she looked like she was really enjoying it, so I carried on and gave her the glass of champagne, praying fervently that she wasn't sick before the drug that I'd put in it would have a chance to take effect. I switched on the music. Ravel's *Bolero,* hardly original but I didn't get to write the scripts and she wouldn't take it out of the book, although I did ask her to twice, before we published.

She drank the wine, ate the proffered strawberries and allowed me to fix two large red fruits to her nipples with cream. It was while I was pouring chocolate sauce onto her exposed private parts ... (and my God but they should have stayed that way, I mean who would tattoo 'come on in boys' down there?) ... that she gave a little sleepy sigh and sank down into the water, her nose and mouth almost submerged. I let a little more water into the bath and then a little more, until she was totally immersed and then I went back downstairs and set the scene in the rest of the house, just like in her book.

It took a good half hour, then I went back upstairs to find that she was completely still, wet and very dead.

I sighed with relief and made my way back downstairs and exited very quietly, via the conservatory at the side of the house.

Seven

Caroline was the first to ring. 'My God Alex – have you heard?'

'Heard what?' I asked, clawing my way across my bedside table to reach my watch. I looked at the time and groaned. 'Caroline it's 6.30 in the bloody morning and its Sunday bloody morning at that!'

'Switch on the local news you idiot.'

I reached over to the other side of the bed and fumbled around until I could turn on the radio; I twiddled a knob and prepared to snuggle back down under the duvet.

'Well?' The phone shouted.

I picked it up, shouted 'Well what?' and put it back down on its shiny plastic holder. Then I went back to sleep.

* * *

I was woken by the doorbell. It was 7.30am and I was not a happy bunny, which is why I wasn't looking my best when I opened the door and Caroline stormed in.

'Will you get something decent on?' she snapped.

'These are decent.'

'Polka dot pyjamas at your age, with pink fluffy slippers, are not ideal wear when answering the door.'

'It's half seven on a Sunday morning so why should I care what I wear to answer the sodding door in?' I snapped back.

'Leonora is dead!'

'*What?*' I stared at Caroline with my mouth hanging open.

'Leonora has gone and gotten herself murdered in some sex game that went horribly wrong.'

'Oh ... how the hell did you find out?'

'The same way you would have if you'd listened to the news like I asked you to,' Caroline barked before trundling down the hall to my kitchen.

'Do you have anything to eat? I'm starving,' she groaned, peering in the fridge.

'No idea, but please don't let that stop you,' I answered before climbing back up the stairs to my bedroom.

'Don't you dare go back to sleep!' Caroline shouted up the stairwell.

'As if,' I muttered, clambering back into my nice warm and smelly pit and pulling the bedclothes up and over my head.

When I finally emerged from my room an hour or two later, dressed in jeans and a baggy rugby shirt, Caroline was hard at it in my office, knocking the stuffing out of my keyboard.

'Well,' she said, surveying the ensemble, 'that's marginally better.'

'Thanks, I think. Any coffee left?'

'There may be some still in the jar.'

'I'll make us a fresh pot shall I?'

'Yes.'

No please, or thank you, and when I entered my usually pristine kitchen it looked like it had been attacked by a rabid herd of elephants on some form of Class A drug. It took a while to locate everything and I returned to my office to find my usually calm and efficient right hand shouting obscenities down the phone.

'You, missy, have had way too much caffeine already,' I advised as I gently replaced my telephone and settled a steaming cup of coffee beside her. She looked up at me and sighed.

'Leonora is dead.'

'Yes I know.'

'Er?'

'You told me, remember, when you almost beat my front door to death.'

'Ah, yes, sorry about that.'

'Oh well, what's the cost of a new paint job between friends.'

Caroline took a long gulp of coffee and then started again. 'The thing is, Leonora is dead.'

'So you have said, many, many, times,' I agreed, sipping at my own mug.

'Listen to me very carefully as you still don't appear to get it. I have rung Shelley.'

'Right?'

'And you still don't know what I'm talking about?'

'Er?'

'Leonora is dead!' At this point Caroline shouted it in my face and slammed her mug down on my desk, spraying a few bank statements with brownish drops, which gave them a slightly Jackson Pollock look.

I looked into my mug for inspiration and tried to focus.

'Alex what the hell is up with you?'

'Leonora is dead.' Because I killed her, I almost added but didn't, which is why I was so tired; only having three hours' sleep can do that to a body.

'Exactly, so I rang Shelley and told her, and she said we could use the cover she has already done, the one we commissioned and Leonora originally agreed to.'

'Right.'

'I've finalised everything. I've sent the text pdf to the printer and the cover went ten minutes ago, they can get the cover printed and the book bound as soon as we check the cover proof, which means ... '

I stared at her: the woman was a genius. 'We can have the book out in three weeks.'

'Maybe two ... '

'Make a killing out of the fact that she died horribly and reprint the book the killer got the idea from so that ... '

'Everyone can read how horrible it actually was ... '

'Genius or what!'

We sat and stared at each other and then we grinned like naughty schoolgirls.

'Book sales may actually go up,' I tentatively suggested.

'And that is why I've tripled the original order and got a brilliant price ... '

'But ... I can't pay for it.'

'Did a deal, extended credit for a month after we launch.'

'How?'

'Don't ask.'

I blinked.

Caroline stretched, yawned and scratched her left armpit. 'God but I'm knackered,' she moaned.

'You can use the guest room if you like,' I suggested.

'Great, thanks, don't mind if I do.'

I thought about what we had done each in our own way and sighed.

'What?' Caroline asked one foot on the first step of the stairs.

'Do you think that we should be talking like this?'

'Like what?'

'Making money from someone's death.'

'Why not?'

'Well ... '

'Oh come on Alex, no one liked her, she screwed you out of every penny she could when she was alive and she was a right royal pain in the ass to everyone she met into the bargain.'

'Well if you put it that way ... '

'Exactly! Its a win-win situation, with no possible down side.'

I agreed with her of course, right up to the point when the police came knocking on my door an hour later.

* * *

This time the Spanish inquisition was held at my home and the inquisitor wielding the thumbscrews was a local chap called Derek. I knew this because he'd introduced himself when he'd turned up to Marcus's funeral. He was accompanied by a tall, rangy, gap-toothed, rather horsey-looking woman who introduced herself as Angela Wainewright. Detective Inspector Angela Wainewright.

I let them in, made some more coffee and prepared to lie to the teeth if necessary.

'So' Ms Wainewright stated, 'you knew the deceased.'

'Yes, she was one of my authors.'

'And how many of these authors do you have?'

'About twenty in all, I guess.'

'And did you like her?'

'Who?'

'Leonora Midora, the deceased.'

'Not particularly.'

'And that bothered you?'

'No, I just published her books, I didn't have to like her, to do that.'

'And was she any good, as a writer I mean?'

'She was all right, wrote middle of the road, bodice-ripping stuff.'

'Some of it was a bit rude though, wasn't it?'

'Well yes ... I suppose ... thing is that's what the public expects and it's not as if it isn't out there ... I mean you can't pick up a glossy mag without something nasty slipping out between the advert for posh knickers and pearlised lip gloss. And don't get me even started on the stuff they stick on the small screen. I mean have you seen *Eastenders* recently?'

'I don't suppose you have a copy of her book.'

'Well her latest hasn't been published yet ... '

'No, I meant the one before that.'

'Why?'

'Do you have a copy?'

'Yes, in the storeroom. I'll go get you a couple.'

I returned five minutes later clutching several copies, to find Caroline sitting in my chair and conversing avidly with the police.

'Will these be enough?' I asked, handing the copies over.

Angela smiled sweetly and then started flicking through the pages. When she got to page 31 she said, 'Oh my, oh my' and by the time she had read through to page 40 she was speechless.

She turned and looked at us, her eyes as round as saucers. 'Just exactly how many of these have you sold?'

'I don't really know,' I replied thoughtfully. 'But off the top of my head about five thousand.'

'Only that many?'

I bristled with indignation. 'Have you any idea how hard it is to sell that many books?'

'Er, no.'

'Well let me tell you that according to the Nielsen figures ... '

'The what?'

'You know the barcode on the back of the book, the one that has the price etc in it?'

'I guess.'

'Well the barcode includes an index number which every published book should have and every year Nielsen can give you the sales figures for each one, scanned and sold through the shops.'

'Ok, got that.'

'Good, well in 2007 out of 85,000 new books, that's brand new not reprints or anything, 58,000 sold an average of 18 copies each in a year.'

'Bloody hell, that's ... not a lot,' Derek muttered, looking at his superior. He looked a bit stunned and for a fleeting moment I wondered if he was writing his memoirs or, even worse, a crime thriller.

'Well if it's that low, why do you bother?' Angela asked.

'Good question and one I ask myself on a daily basis. But the truth is that every publisher has a dream, the dream of the golden goose ... the one writer who will hit the bestsellers list, sell hundreds of thousands of copies and keep on selling them.'

We sat in silence and I could see from Caroline's expression that she to was thinking of the profits on 100,000 copies at £7.99 each even after the usual trade discount.

'Of course the golden goose has to be able to repeat the performance,' Caroline added.

'Ah yes, and your goose has gone and ... '

' ... had itself well and truly stuffed,' I thought.

' ... died on you,' Derek muttered with a glance at Angela.

'Just like that Marcus Foolstop,' Angela added in thoughtful tones whilst looking me straight in the eyes before glancing over at Caroline. 'Foolstop – was that really his name?'

'I have no idea, I just signed the cheques over to him and he wrote the manuscripts using it.'

'Oh.'

I felt a little pity tugging at the corners and smiled back at her. 'But I did always wonder ...'

She grinned back and then I realised that Derek had gone very quiet.

'Marcus Foolstop?'

'Yes.'

'Didn't he drown?'

'Well yes. He apparently jumped from a train, or at least that's what you lot said,' Caroline stated with a shrug. 'Does it matter?'

'I don't know, it's just a bit curious that just recently two of your writers have died and both by the same means. '

'But the radio said that Leonora had died when a sex game had gone horribly wrong,' Caroline interjected.

'Yes and it went horribly wrong in the bath, which was full of water and she drowned.'

'But how can you have sex in the bath with ... '

'You did both read this book?' Angela asked, thrusting the relevant page in front of me. I backed away and glared at her.

'Of course we read it, several times, it got a bit boring to be perfectly honest. And frankly I thought that she made up all the extra curricular stuff.'

'Not according to her current husband she didn't.'

'Really?' Caroline asked with interest, her eyes lighting up with something approaching malice.

'Oh yes, Ms Midora was very keen on her research and apparently liked her sex as kinky as she could get it. She even had one of those rubber S & M suits hanging up in her closet. Made to measure to, or so I'm told, with one of those very heavy price tags.'

'Oh.' Caroline and I exchanged a look of amusement at the thought of the usually elegant and rather prissily dressed Leonora as Miss Whiplash.

'Look there is something you both ought to know ... ' I sighed and then at a very slight nod from Caroline jumped right into my best confessional mode. 'Leonora's last book was actually a bit too near the knuckle and well to be perfectly honest, I – we – were in two minds about publishing it. Then Leonora said that if we didn't she knew someone who would and so ... '

'She blackmailed you into it.'

'Sort of.'

Angela exchanged a knowing look with Derek and stood up.

'Can I keep these?' she asked, picking up the copies of Leonora's last book.

'Yes.'

'And I don't suppose I could have a look at the new one?'

'Well ...' I looked at Caroline who shrugged and then I went over to my desk, opened one of the drawers and extracted one of the copies we kept for review purposes. Carefully and a little reluctantly I handed it over.

'Look, I know that this is no J.K. Rowling but it's not out for a couple of weeks so could you both just be careful who you show it to?'

'Need to know basis only?'

'Okay.' I smiled at that and sat back down in the guest chair.

Angela and Derek moved towards the door and at the doorway paused and looked back at us both, as we sat there glumly looking at Leonora's latest racy novel.

'The crack about being blackmailed,' Angela advised.

'What about it?' I asked.

'Don't worry about it too much.'

'Why ever not?'

'Well ... according to her husband, the ex-husbands we have managed to track down , her housekeeper, the lady that cleans, the young chap who walks her dogs, her children, her driver and several of her friends, Leonora blackmailed them all to a lesser and greater extent. Oh, and just in case you still feel guilty I haven't, as yet, interviewed anyone who even vaguely liked her.'

'Oh,' Caroline and I both said, a trifle stunned.

'So it wasn't just us then?'

'No, not at all. Don't get up, we can see ourselves out.'

Needless to say, I levered myself out of my chair and made sure that they had actually left. And as I watched them drive off in their unmarked car I realised something. They had put two and two together and come up with the fact that two of my writers had recently drowned.

I went back to my office in a thoughtful frame of mind.

To lose one writer might be considered unlucky but to lose two looked like sheer carelessness.

Eight

And then I found myself attending yet another funeral although everyone looked a lot happier than at Marcus's. Leonora's family appeared to have pulled out all the stops, even to the point of having a pink hearse. When I saw it draw in to the rather quaint little church as Caroline was parking the car, I actually wondered if for some reason my new contacts were playing up. Normally I'd have worn glasses to a funeral, as it's terribly embarrassing if you start blubbing and one of the wretched things fall out and I couldn't think of anything less likely to impress than scrabbling around under the kneelers looking for a lens during the eulogy. However I had absolutely no intention of crying at this one. Caroline arrived a few minutes later with her mouth open, I told her she looked like a stunned mullet or possibly a large carp.

'It's pink,' she said, aghast.

'I know.'

'*Pink.*'

'Yes.'

'Oh my God but it's pink!'

'Caroline, remember where we are.'

'Ooops ... er ... sorry vicar.'

The vicar, who had trundled past at that very moment, stopped, muttered that it didn't matter, then turned and stared as we had, except he resembled a ginger codfish.

'Oh dear me, oh my goodness, it really is pink.' The vicar boggled, his eyes standing out on the proverbial stalks.

We stood and openly gawped as the back door opened and the coffin came out. It too was a brilliant, glorious, flamboyant, bright pink, the colour favoured by Barbie and small girls under seven and possibly older ones who have never actually matured past that age. It had gold handles with huge and elaborate white and gold tassels.

'What the he– ' The poor vicar, now almost the same shade, caught himself just in time and then he looked terribly, terribly embarrassed and almost ran inside clutching some sort of overlarge lacy white doily.

'That vicar swore,' Caroline stated, still staring as the funeral director and pall bearers then tried to manhandle the coffin out of the hearse and into the porch, almost knocking over a very large and completely over the top arrangement of stargazer lilies and accompanying trailing greenery.

'Well wouldn't you?' I mumbled as we followed behind the coffin, which had now managed to wedge itself in the corner. There was a bit of a hiatus as the coffin was backed out, we were allowed in and the flowers were removed to one of the side windows.

We blinked in the gloomy interior of the ancient church and found ourselves in the midst of many friends and associates. Leonora's ex-husband Lawrence, her ex-husband Tony and the current one called Wayne, all greeted us with smiles and we were each handed a very large champagne cocktail with a frozen strawberry in the bottom.

Caroline and I exchanged a look and took a tentative sip at the same time; it was absolutely delicious.

'Yummy,' said Caroline.

'Scrummy,' I agreed and then we found somewhere to sit.

The service started with the coffin coming down the aisle accompanied by the grieving family, who spent some time getting to their seats at the front as they'd stop every now and then to shake hands, say hello and discuss the shooting, fishing or general tormenting of small furry, finned or feathered creatures. It was like something out of a P.G. Wodehouse story, the one about that family that shot gnus. I told Caroline and she agreed and I made a mental note to look it up when I got home.

There was a hymn of sorts, one of those chirpy modern things that you can clap to. Someone actually did, he was standing at the back with a young girl dressed as a hippy clutching a tambourine.

After the hymn there was a very short sermon from the vicar on the lines of she was born, she lived and then she died. A prayer or two, also mercifully short as Caroline and I were beginning to get the giggles and then instead of a hymn they played one of the tunes from The Wizard of Oz, the one that went 'Ding Dong the witch is dead'. By then everyone was well on the way to being a little tight and so we all sang along to it, even to the point when a bunch in the middle were singing a four part harmony to the chorus.

The vicar couldn't make up his mind at first whether to be mortally offended until Wayne whispered something to him, and then he went a shade pinker, opened his mouth and sang along in a rather good tenor voice.

Apparently and according to Caroline who could lip read, something to do with having a deaf aunt she was very fond of, Wayne had said and here I quote verbatim 'The coffin and the hearse were Leonora's choice, this however is mine.'

After that we all trooped back outside and watched the pink horror being lowered into the ground, words were said as befitted the occasion such as Good riddance to bad rubbish. Caroline and I stood around and gossiped and then we were all invited back to Wayne's house for the funeral meats.

When we got there we realised that Wayne had definitely had the decorators in, it was pink everywhere.

I blinked upon arrival and put my sunglasses back on, as we wandered as quickly as we could through the house and into the large walled back garden. There was the chef from the Pink Panther tending a huge barbecue, there was a five-piece jazz band and an enormous bar with three barmen.

Waitresses fluttered around bearing trays of roasted meats, sliced bread and interesting-looking salads and things on sticks.

I picked one up and looked at it.

'What's this?'

'I think it's a sausage,' Caroline replied as she prodded a canapé with her index finger.

'It's got stuff on it, pink stuff.'

'So's this. Hang on ... asparagus, pink asparagus, but quite nice really.'

I bit into the little organic pork thing, it was really very good.

'Grain mustard and something sweet, could be marmalade of some kind.'

We looked at each other. Then we looked across at Wayne, who was draped over one of the barmen.

'Well!' Caroline exclaimed. 'That would certainly explain a lot.'

'It would indeed,' I agreed.

After the canapés had been eaten and the food went back to a more normal colour, on the grounds that Big Tony, the Chef from the Pink Panther Café, had promised to stick the bottle of red food colouring Wayne had given him, where the sun wouldn't shine and with extreme prejudice, the funeral went from festive to fiesta in a very short time.

Several hacks and some of the more well-known faces of the literary world, ones that managed to appear regularly at book festivals and on those rather trying art programmes, cornered me either going or coming back from the bar with little snippets of gossip and promises to look favourably upon Leonora's last offering. One even said that he though she was all set to acquire cult status. Or at least that's what I sincerely hope that he said.

I smiled and grovelled and somehow managed to stay fairly sober, well all right then, fairly upright but not at all sober.

Caroline and I eventually left rather hurriedly when Wayne though it would be a good idea if we had a big bowl and threw our car keys in.

'You know Caroline old pal,' I said as the taxi driver hauled us away from the pink palace.

'I think we may actually have our first bestseller.'

'And the icing on the cake is that the wicked witch is dead.'

'Most defini .. inen ... tely.'

'You're drunk.'

'So are you.'

'Alex, oldest and bestest friend, can I stay the night, I really don't think that I can go all the way home without throwing up at least once.'

'Sure, be my guest, I even have a room for it and ... '

'What?'

'It's not even the littlest bit pink.'

I think we both managed to get back to my place and the taxi driver was kind enough to open the front door for us. He said it was nae problemo besides which he'd only just had his car valeted.

Caroline and I grabbed a glass and a very large bottle of mineral water, plus a packet of Nurofen each and repaired to our separate rooms where we snored loudly until the following morning. Groggily and very slowly in case my head fell off I negotiated my way downstairs, switched on my computer and was informed that we had hit number 78 on the UK bestsellers list.

Nine

It was a month after the funeral and Caroline was going through a new manuscript with me. Since we had hit the list, I'd been inundated with orders and we'd had to reprint twice due to deals with both Waterstones and Smiths. The wholesalers Bertrams and Gardners were our new best friends and we were even in the process of sending a pallet load of books to a wholesaler in the Isle of Man. Things had gone ballistic and I wasn't really sure that I was in any way prepared for it.

'You know what you need?' Caroline said as she observed me from over the top of her reading glasses.

'What?' I was marking a typo in in red and wasn't really listening.

'Will you listen to me?' she shouted.

You see that's what best friends are all about, knowing when to ignore what you say and just yell until they get your attention.

I put the pen down, crossed my arms and waited for what ever it was that needed my undivided attention before it hit the proverbial fan.

'Alex, you need to sort all of this out.'

'All of what?'

'That.' She pointed at the heap of paperwork mulching in a large wooden box, which had previously held a rather decent red I'd found in the backwoods of Burgundy.

'We can't go on like this, you know.'

There were more invoices than I could shake a stick at, and even more turning up every day, and someone had to deal with the foreign rights which now looked very lucrative indeed. I had a couple of school sixthformers turning up after school to batch up the books and the post office were even sending a van round to collect all the boxes. The DHL courier was now on first name terms. I had been asked to go on several radio chat shows; I even had my own weekly programme where the presenter and I, with the help of a guest writer or two praised or slagged off anything in the literary firmament. I was going to a couple of festivals as a guest speaker and had an offer of being MC on a cruise liner in the Med. What I didn't have was the time to do any of it!

'Yes I know, but what do I do?'

'Nothing, because I've already done it,' Caroline smiled. I noticed that she smiled a bit like that crocodile in the *Just So Stories* and my heart quaked.

The doorbell rang and she got up with a spring in her step and hared off to greet our visitor before I'd had time to lever myself out of my chair.

And then she came back with the Terrible Trudy in tow.

'Alex, meet your new managing assistant,' Caroline announced and then left us together as she wafted off to the kitchen to make a pot of tea.

We glared at each other, or rather I glared and Trudy looked around at the mess.

'And not a moment too soon by the look of things,' Terrible Trudy observed, heading straight for the wine box.

'What is all of this?'

'Yesterday's invoices, correspondence, new manuscripts, bills, job applications and the annual return plus a list of stuff to do for next week.'

'And all the rest?'

'What rest?'

'The stuff before yesterday.'

'Oh I've done all of that. It's filed in those big cabinets, individual folders for each company, writer, enquiry etc. The bank statements were reconciled up to last Friday and they're in the big purple box file.'

'Oh.'

There was a pause as I sat back down, took off my glasses and rubbed my eyes. She wandered to the cabinet, took a look through and then whistled.

'What?' I asked.

'How did you find the time for all this?'

'I dunno, I just keep going until it's all done.'

She looked at me a little oddly and then Caroline came back with the tea and a plate of biscuits. I poured myself out a large cup, added two sugars and grabbed a biscuit. It wasn't until I'd nearly finished my tea and biscuit that I noticed that they were both staring at me.

'What?'

'When did you last eat?' Trudy asked and actually for once didn't look a bit terrible.

'Er ... I had a sandwich last night.'

'No. I meant when did you last have a proper meal.'

'Not counting Leonora's funeral?'

'No, not counting the funeral.'

I sat and pondered for some time, until I remembered. "Um ... it must have been the day before the funeral, because I had wilted spinach and a steak with blue cheese sauce. I love blue cheese sauce.'

I sighed and reached for another biscuit.

'That was a month ago Alex!'

'I told you,' Caroline murmured.

'Look Alex ... may I call you Alex?'

I nodded, she seemed to be on a roll and it would have been rude to interrupt besides which while she was talking I could eat more biscuits.

'You have dragged this poor benighted kitchen industry into the century ... '

'Of the fruitbat ... ' I felt as a Pratchett fan that one ought to mention it apart from which Caroline for some unfathomable reason thought he was pretentious and my quoting little bits always annoyed her.

'Er yes ... kicking and screaming ... '

'Definitely screaming, not sure about the kicking bit.'

'Right. I've looked at the figures and we are looking at about half a million, possibly more ... '

'Turnover – really?' I perked up.

'No.'

'Oh.' I slouched.

'Net profit.'

I sat up and goggled at her.

'Possibly more.'

I gulped.

'Yes.'

'Oh.' It isn't often that anyone manages to render me speechless but Trudy had managed it in a matter of moments and with two little words, 'net' and 'profit'.

'You and Caroline have done sterling work to get it to this point without falling apart but – '

'Alex, I just can't do it any more,' Caroline sighed. 'Do you remember Suzy and Charlie?'

I shook my head.

'They are my children, Alex, and you are their godmother. Do you remember Jerry? My husband, he's stuck a photo of me on the kitchen window sill and every day after he picks the kids up from their grandmother's or the after school activity, he shows it to them and says this is what mummy looks like. '

I stared at her aghast; I had absolutely no idea things had gone that far.

'Alex look at yourself, go on upstairs and take a good hard look and then tell Trudy that you don't need her.'

I glared from one to the other and swallowed hard.

'So' I said, 'just exactly what will you do and more importantly, why?'

Trudy sucked in her bottom lip and then after a bit of thought told me that she didn't like banking, the bank or other bankers, which must have been a bit tedious for her, and probably accounted for the sour 'I've been sucking lemons all night so don't mess with me face' she always wore whenever we met.

She then produced a large pad of paper from a handbag that resembled the portmanteau that Mary Poppins had and proceeded to tell me what she was going to do.

'First you need a full time administrator-cum-manager, someone to sort out the paperwork and ensure that the orders go out every day and if necessary employ more part-timers and someone to take control of the warehouse.'

'Warehouse!' I squeaked.

'Yes Alex, you can't keep them all in the garage.'

'But I moved the car out, and it's double-skinned, so perfectly dry.'

'There is no room for the packers, Alex.'

'Look during the hotter weather they can pack outside and ... ' I had a bit of a think and then had a brilliant idea. 'What about the potting shed?'

'No.'

'Oh,' I had a momentary sulk and then remembered that we had a new book due in from the printers that week and there wouldn't be room for a small squashed cat, let alone anyone else. 'Fine, we get a warehouse.'

'Good, because part of the warehouse can be used as an office, maybe in the loft space.'

'But ... '

'You can't possibly have any more people in this room and still be able to actually work, you'll end up killing someone.'

I stared at her, she had a point.

'You also need a part-time or even full-time accountant and when was the last time you had a look at your own website?'

'We have a website?'

'Yes you do, and that comment answers the next two questions on my list.'

'Oh.'

'The last additional member of staff needs to be a junior and we can probably put he or she in charge of keeping the website updated with all the latest books, handling enquiries and internet orders. We can deal with the rest ourselves. At least that way whoever we take on has something to occupy them right from the start.'

'But what do I do?'

'You do what you're good at, Alex.'

'You look through the new manuscripts and you find us another bestseller,' Caroline chipped in.

'Exactly.'

'And then *I* do what *I'm* good at and get it ready to print,' Caroline then added before I could think of anything to say.

'Right.' I got up and stalked to the door, into the hallway, up the stairs and into my bedroom and stood in front of my wardrobe mirror and looked at what I'd become, a successful publisher.

The woman that looked back at me had bags under her eyes, the size that you could pack for a long weekend, stringy lanky hair, pale spotty skin, and clothes which hung from her shoulders. I'd obviously lost a lot of weight, although I had no idea how much or how. I was, even I had to confess, a complete and utter mess.

I marched back down the stairs and stood in the doorway of my study and looked the Terrible Trudy right in the eyes.

'All right,' I said. 'When do you start?'

* * *

That day for the first time in ages Caroline went home early. Trudy found a warehouse with suitable office space and rang the removal men, and I went and had my hair done.

And by done I mean coloured, cut and blow-dried. Tracey my normal hairdresser tutted around me like a mother hen the moment I entered the salon and took personal affront at what I had done to myself. 'Your roots are showing and not only showing but waving banners and singing songs from the shows,' she whinged and then got to work with the goo.

Two hours later I emerged and toddled off to Debenhams. Two hours after that and thanking the good God in the sky for late night shopping, I emerged blinking into the neon-lit street and headed for one of the swankier hotels. I booked a room with a large executive roll-top bath and then, after the porter had shown me how to use all the switches in the room, including the one that changed the mood lighting in the bathroom and the one that closed the blinds, settled in for the night.

The porter, needless to say, was not included in room service, which was a pity as he looked a little like Johnny Depp in the film *Sweeney Todd*, but the room was wonderful. I had a very large, very long bath, wrapped myself in the complimentary bath robe and ordered my favourite room service meal; steak, big fat chips, salad and a béarnaise sauce with a bottle of sparkling wine and a cafetiere of strong hot coffee.

It had been over a month since Leonora had joined the ranks of the recently deceased and become suddenly famous and I didn't feel even the slightest bit guilty, in fact I was beginning to wonder if I could do it again.

Ten

We moved into new premises with surprising ease, due in the main to my new right hand woman Trudy, who had proved from the start to be exactly what I needed, in fact from the moment that I walked into my study after my luxury overnighter and found her on the telephone shouting at the bank.

'Look I'm not asking you, I'm telling you to get it sorted or I'm going straight round to the Ombudsman. Don't give me that, I know perfectly well that an internal transfer does not take a sodding week! And if necessary I shall come down there with a suitcase, take the whole lot out of the number one account in cash and pay the whole fucking lot back in the number two ... and I'm not swearing ... you want to hear swearing just tell me again why you can't do it until next Thursday when the wages are due on Wednesday ... '

She stared at me as I stood in stately silence in the doorway.

'Who was that?' I asked

'That tit, Colin.'

'The one with the unfortunate nose and sticky-out ears?'

'Officious, stuck-up little bastard.'

'He the one that cut up my Visa card?'

She nodded.

I walked over to my desk, sat down, took the phone off the receiver, punched in the numbers to the bank and waited. After I'd been given the usual run-around by numbers, I finally spoke to a real human and asked for Colin. I waited and then I waited some more, and eventually he answered although he sounded like he had a mouthful of something.

'Colin Farragher here.'

'Ah Colin,' I said in my sweetest voice, 'have you just been speaking to my new assistant Trudy?'

I listened to Colin as he vented his spleen.

'Oh, I am so, so sorry about that. You see what she really should have said is that unless the money is transferred from our number one account in time to cover the salaries paid from our number two account, I will personally come down to the bank with a couple of very large warehousemen and nail your balls to the wall. On the other hand I could just transfer the entire £750,000 to Barclays and then you can explain to your manager where it went and why.'

There was a momentary silence followed by a soft choking noise.

'No problem,' he finally whimpered. 'Consider it done.'

'Good.' I smiled into the phone and put it softly back onto the receiver.

'Now that, my young apprentice, is how you treat a banker.'

'Well I'll go to the end of our street.'

'And now whose roots are showing?'

After that I found that we got on like Bonnie and Clyde, Corbett and Barker and even at times like Jekyll and Hyde.

But most important of all we started making money.

Lots and lots, of lovely money.

And we published books, unfortunately not quite as many as we could have.

In the end I rounded up my more promising writers and offered them real money to cover the lost wages from their other jobs and packed them off, one after the other, to a little place in Scotland where it was very, very quiet. There was only one casualty, Robbie, a nice young man from Tyneside who wrote crime. He found it too quiet, snuck out of the cottage, down the drive and tottered an hour later into the nearest pub where he promptly tried to go through their entire whisky and beer selection. Not a mean feat by and large and he might have got away with it if he hadn't have tried to discuss football with a Celtic supporter from Dundee.

He has since left the local infirmary and in a couple of weeks they will be able to remove the cast from his writing hand, which was a tad unfortunate as he had only managed the first 6,000 words of an 87,000 word novel. He grovelled a bit when he came to see Trudy and myself in the office, especially as Caroline was there and she was wearing her Jean Brodie glasses.

I can still remember the look on his face when I told him that we had found the perfect writers' retreat, a lighthouse perched on a rock in the Irish Sea only accessible by boat and only during the warmer months.

I was actually only joking but he left his full-time job a week afterwards and we lost track of him completely, until that is, we got a postcard from Madagascar.

* * *

I was still wondering what to do about our current dearth of new titles, which was a new and not pleasant experience. In the past I'd had the complete opposite, which was manuscripts I desperately wanted to publish and no funds to do it with. Now we had funds in plenty and not enough in the way of a viable product.

It was while I was inspecting a forty-seven page epic poem about faeries in block capitals with no punctuation whatsoever that Leonora's widower Wayne turned up. He was clutching the hand of his latest squeeze and a large carrier bag from Harrods food hall.

'Well?' I said, looking up briefly, before sighing and filing the offending literary garbage in the bin. It had arrived sans stamped, self-addressed envelope, so what did Desperate from Hartlepool expect?

'Um ... '

'Wayne, "um" doesn't really do it for me now.'

'Er ... '

'Or for that matter, "er".'

'Well ... '

'Wayne!' I snapped.

His friend gave him a nudge and Wayne handed me the bag.

I looked inside and found a manuscript; what is it with writers and food halls?

The title on the front said 'The Frisky Florentine' and then it said below, 'by Leonora Midora'.

I gulped and then with tremulous hands, turned a page and read. I was twenty pages in when I realised that Wayne was stilling standing to attention by my desk.

'Wayne sweetie, find a chair and for God's sake sit in it. You make the place look untidy and don't whatever you do wriggle.' I looked around. 'Where's the appendage?'

'He's gone to make some coffee.'

'Good, we'll need it.'

I turned over a few pages and then I read the end. It was good, in fact it was better than good, it was excellent.

I waited until his other half turned up with the coffee and then I rang Trudy and asked her to come into my office and to bring a cup. She arrived about a minute later clutching a Wallace and Grommit mug, with a slightly risqué but amusing quote on the front, involving a cracker and a small slice of Wensleydale.

I placed the manuscript in front of her, tapped the title page and waited for her reaction. She boggled, then she read the first pages and boggled some more.

'Well,' she said. 'Who would have thought it?'

'We found it in the attic,' Wayne advised.

'In a box,' added the appendage.

'That's right, in the attic in a box.'

The Marx brothers paused and drew breath.

'We wondered if it might be worth something?' Wayne asked.

'It might,' I agreed cautiously. 'And Leonora wrote this when exactly?'

They looked at each other and then smiled straight into my eyes, the lying little toads.

'On our honeymoon, but it's a little bit naughty and so she put it in the attic.'

'In a box.'

'That's right, in a box.'

Trudy had by now reached page eight and nearly choked on her chocolate bourbon.

'A little bit naughty!' she exclaimed and looked at me.

'Now let me get this straight ... ' I said, steepling my fingers and leaning back in my chair. I had the fleeting desire that a white cat should be purchased at some point and then leant forward and fixed Wayne with my very best steely stare.

'You found this in the attic in a box and it was put there by Leonora because she didn't think I would publish it. Now why do you think that she would have thought that?'

'Um ... '

'You see Wayne, I'm a publisher, that's what I do and I would certainly have published that.'

'Oh ... well ... '

'She didn't exactly write it, did she?'

'Not exactly ... she half-wrote it and we found it and then we ... we ... we ... sort of finished it.'

'Sort of finished it?'

'Yes.'

'You finished it from where exactly?'

They both looked a little like very naughty sheep and about as clever.

'Page three,' Wayne whispered although I'm sure that his sidekick muttered 'two'.

'Two, three, which is it?'

'One.'

'So you wrote it.'

'But Leonora did the title and she wrote a plot line see ... '

They handed me a very worn piece of paper covered in Leonora's spidery hand. The plot, such as it was, was very definitely that of the great and recently deceased Leonora.

'Couldn't you publish it – you know with her name on the top? No one has to know that we sort of er ... '

'That you are in fact Leonora's ghost-writer.'

'That footballer did it ... Keane whatsits face,' the companion earnestly urged, looking almost angelic.

'He was sued,' I growled before adding, 'What's your name?' I couldn't keep referring to him as the appendage even if he seemed to be almost permanently attached at some point to his 'friend'.

'Who me?'

'Yes you.'

'It's Nigel.'

'Right Nigel,' I paused and bit my bottom lip, a thing I was doing a lot of recently. 'And Wayne, why would I publish this under Leonora's name?'

'Because that's what publishers do isn't it? I mean that Patterson bloke is always publishing books with his name on the front and somebody else writes them.'

'Or helps them, they have their name underneath, only it's smaller.'

'And bloody annoying it is too.' I muttered, as I remembered picking what I thought was the latest Alex Cross from a pile whilst loitering about in some airport. Only to find, when I'd reached the departure lounge, that it was by someone else entirely and that Alex Cross was missing totally and utterly. It was also pants to boot and I left it unread and unwanted on a seat before boarding the plane. Hopefully security would have picked it up and have had it detonated somewhere, which would to my mind have been a fitting end.

'So you don't want it?'

'No. Not under Leonora's name.'

Their faces fell and they sat and held each other's hands in silence.

'I want to publish it under yours, both of your names.'

'But why?'

'Because it's really good.'

'But we thought that ... '

'Yes?' Good grief if they hold hands any tighter they'll break something.

'If you published it under Leonora's name then you could say after a while that it had been ghost-written by us, and then publish our next one straight afterwards.'

'The next one?'

'Yes, this one.'

I sat a little stunned as they handed over another manuscript. It had a rough synopsis at the front and at first glance the plot looked far superior to anything that Leonora could write.

'Just exactly, how many of Leonora's books have you worked on?'

'Er well ... the last one and half of the one before that. I was her assistant you see and she told me that I'd never make it as a writer but that she would train me and – '

'Did she marry you to stop you spilling the beans?'

'Well I suppose so, now I come to think of it but at the time she told me that I'd get everything as her husband and then ... '

'The bitch lied,' Nigel exploded. 'She changed her will and all my Wayne got was the house complete with a bloody great mortgage!'

'It's why we redecorated, to make her a laughing stock, so she'd be remembered as the romance writer with the Barbara Cartland fixation.'

And it worked too. I remembered the pieces that came out in the press after the funeral. The normally tasteful Leonora, who had paid a small fortune for bespoke pieces of modern art and cream design interiors, would have had a fit if she'd seen it.

But what to do?

Trudy got up and moved towards the second manuscript, which she read standing up.

'Oh.' She said between pursed lips. 'This definitely needs thinking about.'

'Do either of you have any money left at all?' I asked.

'Not much,' Wayne admitted

'But we still have each other,' Nigel muttered.

They gave each other another nauseatingly loving look and placed a hand on the other's knee for all the world like a rather twee porcelain figure of two shepherds circa 1720. Or was that a shepherd and a shepherdess?

'Look I'm going to get a contract drawn up and as these are exceptional circumstances, I'm prepared to offer a small advance. This is what I'm prepared to pay, but remember this is an advance on sales which means it's a loan.'

'A loan?'

'Exactly and just like a loan, it has to be paid back out of the sales figures, before you get anything else.'

They looked at the number I'd written down and then they looked back at me.

'We'll take it,' said Nigel.

'We can start up that little tea rooms in Lower Snoring,' Wayne agreed.

'And in the meantime you can sort out both of these manuscripts and start on the next. I'll get our legal department to draw up a suitable contract and send it on to you. And then when you've signed it I'll forward you the cheque.'

'Oh thank you, thank you.' Wayne and Nigel bowed their way out, not unlike someone bowing to the Great Oz, a thought that popped into my head almost at the same time as Trudy started humming a tune from the same musical.

'So what did Little Comfrey's answer to Jedward want?' Caroline asked five minutes later, as she popped her head round my office door.

'Now it's funny that you should bring that up, because we need to talk and then I want you to read something.'

Eleven

We sat in the gloaming of a warm Edinburgh night, Caroline, Trudy and myself, drinking cocktails and admiring the gradually glowing skyline. It had been Caroline's idea to go to the cocktail bar at the top of Harvey Nicks and Trudy's to stay there past the first and then the second drink.

It had been a good Festival all in all. Wayne and Nigel had been launched onto an unsuspecting public, first as the ghost-writers of Leonora's posthumous book and then, as they emotionally 'fessed up', to the one she had written before she died. At that point they had become the darlings of the media, which as you know is fickle at the best of times and downright satanic at the worst.

Now they could do no wrong and were being hailed as the latest thing. Both of them had become best friends with most of the literati thronging the writers' and invited guest tables at the Book Festival in Charlotte Square. You must have seen them, they're the ones cordoned off by chains and thick ropes, complete with posh umbrellas and comfortable cushions. I'd already spotted Ian Rankin sporting a modishly outrageous shirt, complete with pink flamingos and for some reason lime green palms with purple coconuts, talking conspiratorially with Stuart McBride. Perhaps they were swapping helpful and handy hints about various nefarious deeds and the right way to decapitate an agent – who knew? – but every so often they would look up as if scanning the area for someone or something.

Patricia Cornwell hove into view, trailing a coterie of 'yes' men and women and both writers disappeared so quickly that they could have been a pair of merkats.

Caroline and I exchanged glances; we were, after all, merely the back-room boys and not the stars and therefore not important enough to be targeted by the celebrity writers themselves but only by those who aspired to join them.

'So how many did you get?' I asked idly, whilst wondering if either of the aforementioned rather tasty Scottish writers wore the kilt and if they did, whether the traditional rumour was true.

'Ten, but one didn't count as she gave it to me, to give to you.'

'Largish woman, bright orange hair, very, very thin legs?'

'Wore black lipstick and enough beads to make an art deco brothel lamp from scratch?'

'One and the same.'

'Wanda!' We both screeched in unison.

'That was almost an eldritch moment,' Trudy observed as she stood beside us and watched the assembled hoard queuing for various tents. 'And how come you both know her?'

'Every year Wanda hands us her new manuscript and it's always almost exactly the same as a recent bestseller.'

'Right, so why not tell her to go away?' Trudy asked.

'Because one day, she might write it before the bestseller comes out and then we offer her a contract and beat the trend,' I replied.

'What is an eldritch moment?' Caroline asked.

'It's something Shakespearian ... or maybe Pratchett,' I replied.

'In other words some bugger made it up,' Caroline sniggered.

'So, how are our two heroes of the hour doing?' I was still counting manuscripts in my head. 'Damn, you beat me by one. '

'Beat you ... what?' Trudy asked.

'Caroline and I have this competition between us to see who gets given the most unsolicited manuscripts at any festival event or literary evening. Usually I win but for some reason today is the day of the editor.'

Queue drum roll. Caroline bowed quaintly in all directions and then offered to buy the drinks somewhere exotic, which is why we ended up sitting in the very swish cocktail bar at the top of Harvey Nicks and enjoying the view over the rooftops of Edinburgh's New Town, castle and some column with a huge man on the top. At least I think it was a man, on the other hand I'd had a few drinks and no food, so it may have been a horse standing on two legs.

'What do you do with them?' Trudy asked, whilst gamely trying to stab a cherry with her cocktail stick when she was clearly beginning to see two of everything.

'Do with what?'

'The manuscripts.'

'We keep them for a bit and then we have a look, bin those we don't like the look of ... '

'Or who can't be bothered to edit their own work ... ' Caroline groaned and clutched at her temple.

'Or, as Quasimodo there said, can't be bothered to edit their own work ... and then we may offer to do something with what is left.'

'We don't bin all of them.' Caroline added hastily, suddenly feeling guilty; she usually feels guilty about something after one or two drinks and tonight she'd had at least four. 'If they come with an envelope we send them back.'

'Course we do, always do that, rude not to,' I agreed and wobbled.

'You know, I think someone must have put something in my drink,' I pointed out, waving my little paper umbrella in the air. 'And it's a bloody blue one. What have I always said about drinking?'

Caroline and Trudy thought deeply and then in unison and a sing-song voice recited, 'Never drink anything blue 'cos after one you're under the table and after two under the host.'

'Exactly.'

I then fell off my stool and we had to be helped to the lift by one of the bar staff. I say we, because Caroline, Trudy and I clung to each other in a line and as long as someone sober acted as a pit prop we were generally speaking all right, until we got to our individual hotel rooms and had to separate. The other thing we realised as the staff helped us down the lift and out of the side door was that it really was a bit late in the evening. I say this because as we were politely manhandled through the door, the shrubs in two very smart containers on either side of the outer door were hauled back inside, and the door was very firmly shut on the outside air and on us.

This year the expense account was in tip-top condition, due largely to the miserly ministrations of our new accountant Hamish, who was a dour Scot from Halifax and made Ebenezer Scrooge look like Sarah Ferguson on a girls' night out. That is, the Ebenezer before the spirits turned up. Anyway due to being in funds and having worked really hard to get Wayne and Nigel onto the public bookshelves, we had treated ourselves to the Sheraton Grand and in particular to unlimited use of the spa suite. I was almost addicted to the aroma steam room and the wonderful and enormous rooftop hot tub.

And so it was with a feeling of well-being that I thumbed through my collected manuscripts, discarding the really rubbish ones into the bin by the door and I came across the one with my real name on it.

No, not the name I had been using since I had changed my life but the one I grew up with: Alexander Neville Moncreiff.

I sat and looked at the paper in my hand, fell to the floor and cried and cried and cried.

Twelve

I awoke to find myself wrapped around the toilet pedestal, the remains of my six cocktails still lurking in the bowl, which I hastily flushed.

Blearily I looked around: something was making a funny noise. Something that sounded a bit like a phone. I peered around the room and realised that I could barely see out of one eye which meant that not only had I been very drunk indeed but that I had lost another contact lens. Although thankfully not in the same situations as I had before becoming celibate.

I eventually found the phone, tracking it down by sound and touch. I picked it up and waited.

'Alexander?'

'What? Who?'

'Have you read the manuscript yet?'

'What?'

'I want fifty thousand in used notes or I go to the press.'

'What!' I spluttered.

'You heard.'

Then the phone went dead.

I sat down hard on the side of the bed and then decided that I had better get sober, really, really quickly. I ordered a room service cafetiere of really strong coffee and a steak sandwich with extra steak.

Afterwards I felt better but as the minutes of my life ticked by I realised that Alexander was very, very dead although Alexandra was very much alive.

The phone rang at two in the morning and it could only be one person and one person only.

'Alexander?'

'What do you want?'

'Gosh a whole sentence, you must be almost sober.'

'Do you accept cheques?'

'Is the Pope a catholic?'

'I bloody hope so or there will be a lot of very disappointed nuns.'

'Funny, but then you were always the clown, eh Alex lad?'

'Stop pissing me about and tell me where we meet to get this over with.'

'Leith.'

'Where in fucking Leith?'

'You really don't need to know where, just get your arse down to the front of the hotel and catch the first taxi you see.'

'But ... '

And the voice had gone.

I hastily grabbed a coat, pulled a woollen hat down over my head and topped the whole lot off with a plain black cashmere scarf. Luckily I'd packed for every possible weather type because although it was August and therefore in theory high summer, it was also Scotland.

I carefully left the room, ensuring that I had my plastic entrance card and made my way towards the lift. And then I stopped – what the hell was I doing? So I went back to the room, carefully wrote out a cheque for fifty thousand pounds and left the payee blank. Then I left my room for the second time and eventually made it to the front door on the first floor and walked off into the night. There was a lone cab waiting outside and I headed straight for it. I got in the back and before I could speak to the driver it was off.

Eventually we reached Leith and the tarted-up docks. I remembered a time when to come down here in the dark you were in serious risk of receiving a good kicking but now ...

The cab stopped and the driver got out and sauntered off towards the water's edge.

There was something oddly and disquietingly familiar about him, something not quite right and it was bugging me so I followed him. He waited in the shadow between two streetlights and lit a cigarette.

'Want one?' he asked, proffering the pack.

'No thanks.'

'Oh I forgot, nice boys like you don't smoke.'

'I have the cheque; it's made out for fifty thousand and I've left the payee blank.'

'You think I'm stupid?' he hissed.

'No, of course not. '

'You must think I'm really stupid ... what you gonna do, wait for the fuckin' bank to open and fuckin' cancel it? What sort of a wanker you think I am?'

I backed off a bit then; he was a nutter and I was in the middle of nowhere with no witnesses and anything could happen.

'You don't even know who I am, do you Alex? Do you, Alexbloodyzander Monbloodycrieff?'

I backed away a bit more and then he lunged at me and I got a good look at his face for the first time.

'Cal?'

'So you do remember.'

Oh yes I did remember. I remembered everything. That final mad fling to see if I was actually straight, gay or whatever. He'd been one of the orderlies in the hospital and before I'd made the decision I'd allowed him to pick me up, take me out and then we'd gone to bed together. He'd gone to bed with Alexander Neville Moncreiff and I'd woken up knowing that I was really Alexandra Helen Thompson. After we parted I went straight back to the hospital, paid the exorbitant fees they charged and put right the mistake that the nurses and doctors had made the day I was born an hermaphrodite.

Unfortunately he had fallen in love and it all got very tearful, very messy, and I'd left him without as much as a backward glance. And now here he was demanding money with menaces.

'Look,' I said, raising both hands in the air. 'I'm sorry, really I am, but I'm Alexandra now and if you want to tell the world, tell them. It isn't after all anything new. For God's sake they had the same sort of storyline on *Coronation Street* a few years ago.'

'You really think I care about some shag years ago?' he hissed. 'You really think you were that good?'

I shrugged, puzzled. 'Look Cal, what do you want?'

'I want fifty thousand now and another fifty thousand on the exact same day every year until you or I die.'

'Get stuffed,' I muttered and turned away.

'How much is your new empire worth, eh Alex? Your new girlfriends might not mind a gender bender like you, but you think that they are going to want to be with a murderer? What about all those little writers? What would they say about you increasing your book sales by knocking them off when they no longer have anything more to write ... surplus to requirements, eh Alex?'

'It was an accident ... '

'Really, you think they are going to actually believe that!'

I went cold inside, my heart raced ... there was no way that he could know about either murder ...

'I was just passing through that village of yours, stopped for petrol and a slash and saw you and that writer leaving the café. I followed you to the station Alex, I saw you push him ... I saw –'

He was going to ruin my life because of an accident and because of a twenty-year old grudge and then I saw red; I saw red the moment he told me what he was going to do with my company and it was then that I realised just how much it all meant to me. All those people that relied on me, all those hangers on, children, spouses, parents ... And he was absolutely right, the moment they found out about Marcus I was doomed. No one would want me to publish them, not if they thought I made a habit of knocking off writers.

There was a length of wood on the ground and it was just a matter of a moment, not even that, to pick it up and lash out with it.

He was still obscenely threatening when I hit him the first time, he went down on the ground and looked up at me and laughed. 'I was wrong Alex, you hit like a girl. A girlie girl who pushed mama from the train baby ... '

I beat him with the stick as the red mist filled every part of me and I kept on until he'd backed to the edge of the dock and with a splash fallen in over the side.

And the splash was the thing that caused me to stop. The second was the light bearing down at me across the water.

I dropped to the ground, my face turned towards the dark and away from the light, head covered, dark long coat, dark jeans, black trainers. The roar of a power boat getting closer and closer, speeding along the edge to the shrieks and screams of the partygoers on board. It nearly hit the dock wall, skimmed along the side, powered into reverse, then stopped momentarily and sped off into the night. I listened as it went and then as I caught the wail of a siren in the distance, crawled to the edge of the wall separating Leith from the Firth of Forth and peered over.

There was no body, nothing but froth and the mangled, minced and sliced remains of something which could once have been human. I sat on the dockside and shivered – another death, another bloody funeral.

I thought about taking the taxi but in the end I decided to make it look like a robbery which had gone wrong. Luckily I'd had my gloves on all the time so there would be no prints. I did see a *CSI* episode where they got reverse prints off a glove. It had something to do with superglue but was pretty expensive, so I had very little doubt that the Scots – always careful with their budgets – would not be too willing to spend more than they had to on the forensics. Besides which, my fingerprints were undocumented and I would be leaving Edinburgh the day after next.

I was of course sorry about it afterwards; I hadn't really meant to lose my temper and I was going to pay him the fifty thousand. But I had my writers to think about, my staff, my ... well, my family.

I broke one of the windows of the cab, left the doors open and dumped the bloodied stick complete with bits of skin and human hair at the dockside. Then I vanished into the shadows and went back to the hotel. Luckily my coat was one of those reversible things and although the inside was a bright and hideous yellow, at least it wasn't spattered in blood. It took an hour to find a taxi and when I did he charged me a small fortune, especially as I realised as I was sitting in it, that I hadn't actually been that far from the hotel, it just felt like it. I returned to my room with my hat, gloves and scarf in my large and capacious pockets and waited until the earliest opportunity to use the pool on the roof.

I ate an enormous breakfast and then I hurried back to my room and my bed where I slept until lunchtime. At three I was back at Charlotte Square with Caroline and one of my newly successful crime writers giving a fairly well received talk on 'The nuts and bolts of publishing, and was it a man's world?' Rather an irony if you consider the circumstances.

That night the coven, as Trudy, Caroline and I were called by Wayne and Nigel, went to a restaurant called Blonde for a fabulous meal. It was on St Leonard's Street and was one of those gems you often find hidden amongst the kebab houses and all-day sandwich shops.

We wined and dined and then walked across the meadows, past the fair and the circus tents to the edge of the green grass where students frolicked and the odd band played ad hoc music to anyone that cared to listen. A clown raced past, closely followed by a large white rabbit checking his watch and an overlarge and slightly portly fairy who was falling out of his bra and sporting a neat King Charles beard and an extremely worried look.

We did consider following them just to see what would happen but decided against it on the grounds that further off we could hear a jazz band playing the blues softly into an Edinburgh night.

Thirteen

We eventually arrived back at work after one flight and a train journey to find the office in an uproar. The computer had crashed two days previously and no one could get the orders off. The administrator we had left in charge had locked herself in the toilet and the packers were running around like a pair of headless chickens. It was then that the computer guy finally decided to turn up and Trudy swore at him, he swore at the computer and everyone swore at the junior who had started the whole sorry mess.

That night we finally finished the Nielsen orders one minute before the witching hour and with instructions not to turn up for work until lunchtime, everyone left one by one, leaving me to switch of the lights.

I watched them toddle off yawning towards their cars, motorbikes and cycles with a feeling almost matronly.

Later I stood in my bedroom and looked at myself in the mirror, I was definitely no longer a girl but somehow had become a woman, a woman of uncertain age. In fact I almost looked like my mother as I remembered her when I was young.

The next morning I put my old and bloodstained clothing in the bin together with various bags of household waste and cleared out the rest of my suitcase. It was then that I came across the manuscript, the one that Morris had emblazoned my name across. Out of curiosity I read it. It wasn't actually that bad, in fact it was really quite good. It even had the cat in it and yes it dealt only with pushing Marcus under the train. It was as I was getting ready to burn it in the fireplace that I realised with a jolt that Cal couldn't possibly have written it. In fact he was, thinking about it, almost illiterate, there were words in there that required a dictionary to spell right and they were all spelt right. Even the grammar was spot on, if a little pedantic in places.

I sat in my study, lost in thought until the sound of the doorbell interrupted my reverie.

When I finally got to open the door it was to find Mrs Coaltit standing on my doorstep clutching a red umbrella and a copy of the manuscript I had been poring over all morning.

Fourteen

We looked each other up and down and then between clenched teeth I invited her in. I sat her in the lounge amongst my collection of books, ancient inherited furniture and mismatched pictures whilst I tottered off to the kitchen to make a pot of tea and to give myself a short breathing space.

I returned with a laden tray to find her still sitting nervously on the edge of her seat and still clutching her frayed-looking manuscript.

'Nice,' she said. 'I like the carpet.'

'Yes, it's a nice carpet.'

'Unusual having a black carpet in a lounge.'

'Doesn't show the burnt bits when the fire spits.'

'Oh well, that's sensible then.'

We sat for a further five minutes while she admired the sofa, the new plasma screen TV, the cocktail cabinet, and the new coffee table: a sheet of glass resting on an elephant's back which she advised me was much more tasteful than the one her youngest had bought at great expense from the local auction house, apparently his plate of glass rested on the upturned and well-rounded bottom of a PVC-clad young lady of negotiable affection, something I gather that she strongly disapproved of as did her paramour the inimitable Albert.

Eventually I asked her what she wanted.

She pointed shyly at the wadge of papers as I reached over to give her a cup of tea and asked me in a faltering falsetto if I'd liked her manuscript. A manuscript which had fairly and accurately portrayed my first brief encounter with murder, accidental or otherwise. I was, I had to admit, temporarily bereft of the power of speech.

'Um, its ... um ... well-written.'

'Is it? Is it really? Only I was a bit worried ... only I knows that your firm only deals with good quality writing and, well, some of the long words I had to look up and I'm hoping that I got them in context but they felt right at the time.' She smiled at me and eagerly accepted the cup of tea from my trembling hands.

'Of course I got the idea after that awful Mr Marcus was found ... '

'After?'

' ... went up to the station and I thought, what if someone pushed him and he clung on and then fell off over the river ... '

'Someone?'

' ... see the tide was out but he wouldn't have known that the river was tidal, I mean some of the locals don't twig and he lived in the city and well, those city blokes, not got the brains they were born with, my Albert says. I did go and do a bit of research, scene of the crime sort of thing 'cos I went to that lecture you gave at the library a few years back ... '

'Library?'

'You was most particular about getting the detail right and adding a comic touch. So I thought what about Marmalade the cat ... '

'The cat!'

'You know, that awful orange thing, that sleeps in the boiler room, supposed to keep the rats down but all you ever do is see him sleep ... '

'Marmalade?'

'Anyway I hope you don't mind that I made you out to be the murderer ... '

SHE

'Only I thought it would add a nice twist ... '

MADE

' ... and well, book sales did increase after he died, didn't they? My Albert said you'd sue but I said ,what young Alex? and ... '

IT

'Then I thought I'd give it to you but you'd gone up North by the time I'd finished sorting out all the spelling mistakes and things so I caught the train up and went to the festival ... '

UP.

' ... the one with all the books. I couldn't get to see you so I gave it to the nice young man at the side of the tent when young Wayne was signing his books with that friend of his ... '

SHE MADE IT UP!

SHE MADE IT UP!

'You did get it dear, didn't you? Only it took months to write and ... '

I shook myself and then got up and went towards her with my hand outstretched. 'To be honest I haven't really had time to read it all the way through but it did look rather interesting. Oh dear, that tea does look rather cold, let me make you a new one.' I hastily picked up her cup from which she had taken not a sip and with alacrity put it back on the tea tray and sped off to the kitchen. As soon as I got there I poured every scrap of barbiturate-laden tea down the drain and grabbing a fresh teapot from the dishwasher, made another pot. She had made it up and I had nearly drugged an innocent, well fairly innocent, little old lady with the very clear intention of dropping her off in the local gravel pit later. 'Alex,' I said to myself as I fumbled for the fresh milk in the fridge, 'this sort of homicidal mania has got to stop.'

It was then that I realised that not only did I look like my mother but I was beginning to sound like her as well and that if I didn't watch it I too would end up going quietly batty in the local equivalent of God's waiting room.

Upon my return Mrs Coaltit beamed a million kilowatt smile and positively shone. 'Oh thank you dear,' she gushed as she accepted a freshly brewed beverage. 'There's nothing like tea made in a proper pot is there?'

'No,' I agreed, 'There really isn't.'

* * *

Later that week Mrs Maria Coaltit signed a contract and started work on a new great crime novel featuring a doctor who bumped off his elderly patients aided and abetted by the local brothel owner. I had no idea how she was going to research the brothel and wasn't sure that I wanted to know, although I had a sneaky feeling that young Jason and the puritanical Albert would be set to work on this particular part of the book.

Albert spent most of his time telling all and sundry how his Maria was going to be the next Agatha Christie and I breathed a sigh of relief. The only fly in the ointment was that if Maria could work out what had happened, perhaps the police would too.

I worried all day and all night until I met the 'police' in question standing in the middle of the roundabout in a slightly puzzled fashion. Albert stood ramrod straight beside him and together they looked at the destruction of the municipal flower bed.

'I don't know what could have done it,' the officer was saying as Albert crossly tutted and tugged at his earlobe.

'Weeeell ... ' said Albert, in the manner of workmen the world over, just before they spit on the ground and then tell you that you need the equivalent profit of the Brinks Mat job to get the new bath in. 'Looks to me like one of them Reliant Robins, you know them three wheelers like on the telly.'

'What?'

'Didn't you watch that Jeremy Clarkson? Must have been the only one in the village not to if you didn't?'

'Jeremy Clarkson couldn't have done this, he lives miles away.'

Albert took a deep, deep breath and then glared up at Constable Macleod before speaking in the carefully clipped tones one would use when trying not to throttle a particularly stupid child. 'I knows that!' Albert hissed. 'All I'm saying is, that one o' them three wheeler cars did all this damage and such. You know, the cars with only three wheels.'

'Right.' Constable Macleod surveyed the scene of devastation and then completely spoilt his look of lofty intelligence by asking, 'Why?'

Albert at that point realised that I was there and rolled his eyes heavenwards before gritting his teeth and continuing. 'On account of the fact that they can't go round a roundabout 'cos they's unstable and falls over.'

'Oh. So's you reckons it was one o' them free wheelers like on the telly.'

'Yes.'

Albert and I exchanged a look of relief which was however fairly short lived.

'Not Mr Clarkson then.'

Albert blinked. 'No.'

Constable Macleod then took out a small pad and pencil from his top pocket and began to make a few notes. He then finally noticed that he had an audience of myself and the hoodie who delivers the local papers and stood up a bit straighter before asking. 'So who else has one of them three wheelers?'

'Sam Parish has that old one he keeps for going out in a Sunday in, mint condition it is too.'

'Sam Parish eh?' Constable Macleod made another note and then put both pad and paper back in his pocket.

'Right then, I'll be havin a few words with Mr Parish.'

The long arm of the law stalked purposefully off and Albert sniggered evilly.

'So ... ' I asked,' looking at the tyre marks which could be seen clearly running through the centre of the floral clock carefully donated by the local Round Table, 'who actually did do it?

Albert looked around to ensure that the representative of law and order was out of earshot and the hoodie and I shuffled a little closer. 'It was our Jason showing off to that bint of his, after we went to that house of ill repute.'

'He took his girlfriend!'

'Look young Alex, it ain't that bad and that Liza makes a right good steak and kidney pie and chips for thems thats waiting besides which that husband o' hers brews a mighty fine pint down in the cellar and what else are they supposed to do with all them lasses, eh? I means they had six girls!'

'Well ... '

'They was giving it out to that lot off the estate for free, much better to get paid isn't it ... part of the service industry when all's said and done ... besides ... '

'What?'

'That Sam Parish beat me with them so-called English marrers of his, last Harvest Festival flower show and I know damn well he cheated.'

'He cheated? How?'

'Bought em off the internet didn't he, only he bought the wrong breed wot only grows in foreign parts, that's why.'

I walked home, a sober and slightly less worried soul, knowing that the village was in the safe and helpful hands of the village idiot and that Old Albert wasn't half as daft as he looked but nearly twice as evil.

Fifteen

I looked at the pile of mouldering manuscripts on my desk and scratched my head again. I'd just come back from a week of sinful inactivity by the side of a Scottish loch and I was still itching. I love Scotland, I love the people, the food, the hidden distilleries, the spectacular scenery, the over-the-top thunderstorms, I even love the rain. Unfortunately there has to be a satanic level to such innocent pleasures and they are small, invisible and have tiny sharpened razors for teeth. I've tried every trick known to man but the traditional Scottish midge always manages to find some way of getting past my defences and partaking of at least a pint or two of blood. This time they appeared to have stowed away in my hair and although I'd washed it twice since I'd come back, once upon arrival in the wee small hours and once that very morning they still didn't appear to have drowned.

'You're back!' Trudy barked as she entered my room and deposited another dozen or so offerings from a public generally obsessed with being the next J.K. Rowling onto my tottering heap of literary hopefulness.

'Thanks,' I muttered as I scratched behind my neck and then in desperation my ears.

'Do you have fleas?' Trudy asked with interest as she watched me trying to reach a particularly crusty bite between my shoulder blades.

'No, worse, midges.'

'Ah.' Thoughtfully she picked up a couple of empty mugs from the end of my desk. 'I thought you said that place you booked had mosquito nets on all the windows.'

'They do, but the average midge takes no notice and wriggles through the holes anyway. They probably have little midgie wire cutters as standard.' I scratched an arm and then the side of my nose.

'That jungle strength stuff works.'

'Does it?'

'Oh yes.'

'Um, well the stuff from that chemist on the corner next to Greggs doesn't.'

'Did you try Loch water? That usually works.'

'Trudy, short of sacrificing my firstborn child at midnight I tried everything! It just didn't stop the horrid little buggers from turning up in full Ninja kit at 2a.m. and they brought their friends. And at that time in the morning I had difficulty lifting the old eyelids let alone a couple of limbs to enable me to battle my way through the undergrowth, clamber down a precipitous lochside and immerse myself in peaty, ice cold water.'

'Ah.'

'Anyway you expect to scratch on a Scottish holiday, it's on par with sipping a quiet single malt and eating freshly caught salmon. Besides which it's almost obligatory to wage war on the foul and filthy beasts, the problem is that I seem to have brought an entire clan back with me, God damn it.'

'Right.'

She wandered away, leaving me with the paper equivalent of the leaning tower of Pisa and returned a minute or two later with a vibrantly coloured bottle.

'Jungle strength. Now go to the ladies and splash it on all over as we have a board meeting in half an hour and Alex ... '

'What?'

'For fuck's sake stop scratching!'

I waited until she had gone, closing the door behind her and then I sprayed myself from head to toe. Too late I realised that the stuff stank and trying not to breathe in I rushed over to my one and only window and flung it open. The smell was truly horrible. I looked at the bottle and sighed, sometimes the cure was worse than the disease. After a few minutes the room cleared and I realised that my head had stopped itching but that the creases behind my knees could do with a good scratch.

'Right half an hour,' I muttered as I went back to the pile, cracking my knuckles on the way. 'Just enough time to sort out this lot.'

The first worthy tome went straight back, and the second, third and fourth. The fifth had no envelope to go back in and the sixth an envelope and no stamps so they both went in the bin. The seventh showed promise so I put it aside to be read by one of our gang of readers and the eighth was handwritten so that went back without my bothering to even look at it.

There were a further three tales of woe, all thinking they were the most original children's story to hit my desk in a hundred years and they were all about a small brown sausage dog who had hilarious adventures and a small cute owner. They got a comp slip and the equivalent of a must try harder note.

The next one had the title 'Night of a Thousand Shags and Only One Broom Cupboard'; unfortunately that was the only good thing about it.

I was almost at the end when Trudy rang and said they were ready, so I flicked the penultimate one open and speed-read the first page. It was about a banker, in the style of an early Archer, but with less plot and slightly less believable characters. That went back into its accompanying envelope but it left me thinking about plots and bankers, until I finally remembered where I'd seen something similar.

'Trudy,' I bellowed, settling myself down in my boardroom seat a minute or so later. 'Where's that manuscript of yours?'

'Which manuscript?'

'The one you let me have a look at during Marcus's wake?'

'Oh, that one ... '

'Yes, that one.'

'Never got around to finishing it ... '

She handed me a pile of accounts and a copy of the sales reports as she shrugged dismissively and started laying out a few pens and notepads.

'Why not? It was pretty good, loads of potential.'

'Was it?'

'Yes, in fact compared to the stuff I went through this morning it was a Barry award winner at the very least.'

'Oh.'

'In fact it was almost good enough for a Theakston's Old Peculiar.'

'What was?' Caroline asked as she bumbled in weighed down with cover designs and a wad of proofs. If you ever want to know why the rainforest is currently the size it is then you need look no further than the average medium-sized publisher, although even when small I could lop down at least two or three trees a week.

'Young Trudy's opus.'

'My what?'

'You know, your baby, the fruit of your imagination, your sacrifice upon the altar of great works, the … '

'Alex, just shut up and will you please, *please* stop scratching.'

I narrowed my eyes and glared at her. She was definitely in denial, one of the true first signs which in my humble opinion normally accompany a better than average writer.

'Don't try and change the subject, I want to see it,' I demanded as I folded my arms across my chest and waited to see what would happen.

'I never got round to finishing it.'

Ah ha, the second sign.

'Why not?'

She looked up from her perusal of the expense account and then wafted an arm around in a vague and hopeless way.

'Because all of this tends to get in the way. I mean it's difficult writing your own when you're publishing other people's. It also … ' she added as an afterthought, 'tends to put you off.'

'Ah.'

'It would be like working in a restaurant all day and then going home and having to cook.'

My mind went back to some of the offerings of that morning, which included '101 Things to do with a Rice

Pudding' and 'The Pigs' Guide to Plums' and conceded that she did have a point.

After that I asked no more and we continued sorting out our empire well past lunch and late into the afternoon until eventually even Caroline gave up the will to make money and we all went home. So I was somewhat surprised when my doorbell rang at nine that evening and when I opened it I found Trudy on the doorstep clutching a bottle of wine in one hand and an M&S bag in the other.

I clutched my old towelling robe about me and beckoned her in. The nights were definitely drawing in and turning cold, so I'd lit a fire earlier on in the lounge, which was just as well as the heating had packed up again.

'This is nice,' Trudy observed, divesting herself of her coat, scarf, bobble hat and gloves.

'Didn't know it was that cold out,' I mumbled, hanging each item over the edge of one of my leather easy chairs.

'It isn't, my heating's packed in.'

Must be catching, I thought.

'Do you want something to eat? Only I was just going to have some supper.'

'That would be nice,' Trudy replied, looking around at my home with interest.

I toddled off and returned about five minutes later with a tray of cheese, bread, cold meat, pickles, two glasses and a corkscrew.

Trudy handed over the carrier bag and then went about opening the wine.

I took a bite of cheese and a tentative sip and then immersed myself in her tale of nefarious goings on down in the strongroom. Frankly I had no idea that bankers had so much fun or were for that matter that imaginative.

There was an entire chapter dedicated to what happened amongst a pile of bearer bonds after the new budget had been announced that left me quite flushed and just a little bit flustered.

I read a bit further and then took another sip of wine before putting it down on the small round table at the side of my chair.

'Um ... '

'What do you think?' Trudy asked, leaning towards me, her face flushed and suddenly very young and almost vulnerable.

What did I think? Where did I start? It was very, very naughty, occasionally extremely rude and really very good or it would be after Caroline and I had got our paws on it. But it was also like finding out that your parents actually had sex after you were born ... quite, quite, shocking.

After a while I settled for the honest approach. 'It's good. Needs work but has real potential.'

'You're just saying that to be nice.'

'Trudy, I'm a publisher, I'm never nice and before you say it, I'm not joking either. Joking to a writer is one of the things that I'd never do, especially over a new manuscript, it's too bloody expensive.'

'Oh.'

'To them it's never a joke.'

We sat either side of the fire and watched the flames flicker. After a while I threw on another log and poured myself another glass, after leaning forward and topping up the one that Trudy was still clutching.

'Alex?'

'Umm.'

'You do know that you can tell me anything.'

Warning, warning ... I carefully put my glass down and turned to look at her; she had on her worried frown.

'Yes ... '

'It's just that you never mention it.'

'Mention what?'

'You know ... '

'Know what?'

'That thing, the thing that you did.'

'What thing?'

I was now really worried and began to look around me for the poker.

It was then that she looked up and I could see tears in her eyes.

'Oh Alex, I wish you would tell me about it, maybe I could help and sometimes you know it's good to talk about it, get it out of the way, be able to move on and ... '

'And?'

'It's not as if you were the only one.'

You mean there was more than me and Mrs Coaltit's imagination pushing Marcus under a train? I don't think so.

'I know all about you Alex, I did a search on you the day you opened your account in the name of Alexandra instead of Alexander.'

I almost sighed with relief and then as the subject matter hit home I couldn't believe it. She knew, she knew and all this time she hadn't said a word.

'But why didn't you say anything?' I asked carefully, nudging the poker to one side with my foot.

'Because I hoped that one day you would trust me enough to do it yourself.'

'Oh.'

'I know that it must have been so hard, the operation and well ... everything ... especially back then and ... '

Her voice tailed off and she was dabbing her eyes with the edge of her sleeve.

'You know I'd do anything for you Alex, don't you?'

Well actually no I didn't, in fact it had never occurred to me that anyone would.

'It must have been so hard. So how long did you know that you were really a woman?'

'From the moment I could think, I suppose.'

'Oh Alex, my poor, poor sweet and wonderful Alex.'

I looked suspiciously into my wineglass and then at the bottle. Trudy was becoming almost maudlin, it was like standing at the gates of hell and discovering that they'd just installed air conditioning.

It was then that I decided to tell her everything. Well everything about my being born with both a vagina and a penis, about my parents' confusion, about the doctors, about mine. The part when I grew up looking like a boy but thinking like a girl. The bit about me discovering about sex with the girl next door but one. The talks with various members of the medical profession, including at least three specialist surgeons and two psychiatrists. The clinic in Holland, the medicine, the operation, the pain. I even told her about my brief and only sortie into the gay world, although I did leave out the bit about beating the little shit to a pulp years afterwards.

She listened and nodded and nibbled at the cheese and then she got up, kissed me full on the lips and then hurriedly left before I could say anything more.

I rubbed my finger along my bruised mouth and listened to my heart pounding.

So that was why she was so upset and had never invited anyone to the staff dinner, it made perfect sense now.

I just wasn't sure what to do about it.

Sixteen

The thing about service stations is that they are the best places in the world to sit if you want to do a Dietrich and be alone. As long as you remember one essential thing: never ever eat anything that calls itself a panini. Well all right, I admit that even I thought that they looked like paninis. They smelt like a panini should, and I salivated in anticipation right up to the time when I bit into one. I even did it again a week later at a different service station because I couldn't believe that something that looked that good could actually taste that bad. Another five pounds I shall never see again.

Oh and why do they serve coffee in buckets? Surely it would be better to serve less coffee but better coffee. Espressos should not come in mugs, they should turn up all dark, bitter and twisted in small wee cups accompanied by a long thin glass of iced water, maybe a freshly squeezed orange or two ... nine-year-old Spanish kids at the roadside manage it so why not a fully trained barista?

I was musing about the failings of the system and wondering idly what books were selling best in the bookshop that I could see across the concourse, and if any happened to be mine, when Caroline plonked herself down in the seat opposite me and proceeded to empty the tray she had carried over from the counter onto my previously uncluttered table.

'What the hell are you doing here?' I asked.

'Could say the same to you,' she answered, pushing a cup of peppermint tea in my direction.

'Don't eat that!' I hissed as she placed the unexploded panini and accompanying pot of tomato sauce down beside her cappuccino.

'Why, what's wrong with it?'

I was about to give her a list when she bit into it. Her face changed from hopeful expectation to outraged disappointment in a fraction of a second.

'Just swallow it quickly and then release.' I advised. 'It's that or choke to death on the remains.'

'Oh my God – what the hell did they do to it?'

I shrugged because the answer to that particular question could only be answered by Beelzebub himself and only after the devil in question had spent at least three hours chilling in a hot tub as I was frankly of the opinion that even the devil wouldn't do things that bad to an inanimate comestible.

'What was it supposed to be?' I asked out of culinary interest.

'Goats' cheese and sweet chilli jam with sliced roasted peppers and rocket,' Caroline answered, reading from the impressive-looking list on the cellophane wrapper.

'What did it taste like?'

'I'd rather not say before the nine o'clock watershed.'

'I thought I'd be safe with red pesto, roasted vegetables and blue cheese, there should have been a bit of chicken as well but I was blowed if I could find it.'

'And?' Caroline asked as she prodded her panini with a fork.

'It tasted of sweet jam or pickle with something that may have died in the middle. I had a bacon and cheese one before that ... which I can't even begin to describe except that although it wasn't that bad it wasn't that good either.'

'Sounds like the story of my life,' Caroline muttered; she was very obviously depressed so I rambled on regardless, hoping that by some miracle she would forget why she had turned up at my table, in my service station and go away so that I could continue to sulk in peace.

'Couldn't taste the bacon or the cheese just the toasted coffin it was in.'

'I'll go get a packet of crisps.' Rats, she wasn't going to go away so I gave up.

'Stay away from the cupcakes,' I sighed and crossed my arms in defeat.

'Why? They look okay.'

'You know how those buns that my little goddaughter made for the fair tasted, the ones that she got the recipe the wrong way round and stuck in four pounds of sugar instead of four ounces.'

'You think that they may be a little sweet?'

'Certain types of diabetics could die after just one bite.'

'I see. Bar of chocolate and a packet of crisps then?'

'Safest option and no stomach pump required.'

She was back in a matter of minutes clutching her purchases, which she proffered and I steadfastly refused.

'Thought I'd find you here,' she muttered between mouthfuls.

I glared at her. 'How? I mean do you double for Mystic Meg or something? Oh God please tell me you haven't had me tagged?'

'Nope, followed you from the office.'

'Oh.'

'So tell me, oh mighty one, what exactly is going on between you and the Terrible Trudy?'

'Nothing.'

'Doesn't feel like nothing.'

'I have no idea what you mean.' And I sniffed.

'You're upset. I can tell.'

'Huh?'

'You always sniff when you're upset and you either lock yourself in your study and try to work yourself to death or you bugger off to God knows where and sulk.'

'I'm not sulking.'

'Are too.'

We sat in childish silence while she waited for some sort of an answer and I sat and waited for her to go away.

We were still sitting there looking like a miserable pair of bookends when Rich the office junior stroke lothario turned up and threw a handful of cheques at us.

'What the hell do you want?' I spat.

'Accounts want this lot signed by lunchtime so that they can get the royalties out in time to catch the post.'

I waved a hand in the direction of Caroline who had opened her packet of sea salt and cider vinegar crisps and was munching away as if it had gained Olympic or at least Commonwealth Games recognition. She was up to at least a bronze standard. 'Why can't she sign them?'

'She already has,' Rich advised, sitting down and eyeing up the congealing panini. 'You going to eat that?'

'Not in this lifetime, no,' I answered, signing away with a pen I'd found in my handbag.

He grabbed the plate at the same time as Caroline grabbed the sauce pot and before either of us could stop him took a large bite, chewed, swallowed and didn't turn green or die. In fact he polished off the entire thing in a matter of minutes and then starting looking around for more.

Caroline had stopped crunching and was looking in disbelief at the empty plate.

'Very tasty, bit chewy though. Think I might get a hot one.' He looked a trifle guiltily at us both and then longingly at the counter still purveying the wretched thing as food. 'You don't mind, I mean it will take another minute or so for you to sign all of them and check 'em against the list.' He fumbled through all of his jacket pockets getting redder and redder as each investigated space revealed everything except the list. 'Oh bugger, I forgot it.'

I looked up from my Herculean task, gritted my teeth and pointed with my pen at the sandwich bar. 'Go,' I ordered. 'Before I can think of any more reasons why I can't add you to the unemployment figures.' Rich looked uneasily from me to Caroline and back again and then backed away, turned and slunk off.

'Tit!' I exclaimed as he disappeared amongst the hungry hordes.

'He may be a tit but he's a cheap tit and in this present economic climate necessary to our continued growth and productivity,' Caroline advised me and then after a short pause began again on the crisps.

'Well at least now we know who eats them,' I observed, dotting an i.

'Yep, must be one of those boy things I keep hearing about,' Caroline agreed. 'Another of life's little mysteries well and truly solved.'

When Rich had returned and I was still ploughing through the pile, under the watchful gaze of a security guard standing by one of the biggest plastic palms I'd ever seen, I asked him why Trudy hadn't signed the damn things.

'Can't', he answered between mouthfuls.

'Why?'

'Cos she's not there.'

'Oh, is she sick?'

'You don't know, do you?' He stopped chewing and looked uneasily from Caroline to myself and back again.

'Know what?'

'You neither of you know what she's done?'

'No we don't,' Caroline hissed at him. 'Which is why we need you to tell us before I let her fire you, even though I know that it will make the legal department cry into their morning hemloch.'

'But you must know,' he argued, pointing at me with the remains of his soggy toasted panini. 'I mean you must know 'cos you're the boss and you know everything.'

The lad wasn't a tit, he was the village idiot. I took a deep breath and fixed him with my best gimlet stare, I even used the voice. 'Well this time I don't.'

'Ah.'

'For God's sake lad spit it out! What exactly did Trudy do? Set off the fire alarm, pinch the petty cash, set light to the filing ... I mean she did threaten to the last time she couldn't find the invoices for March ... '

Caroline unwrapped the chocolate and winked at me. 'Perhaps she really did nail Colin's balls to the wall with his own staple-gun?'

I grinned at her and then we both turned and glared at the unfortunate Rich who was now squirming with embarrassment. 'She ... she ... '

'Oh come on Richard lad, spit it out, it can't be that bad.'

'She handed in her resignation, cleared her desk and left.'

We both sat too stunned to move.

Trudy had left.

One of the three amigos had thrown in her sombrero, picked up the reins of her trusty steed and ridden off into the distance leaving us to an empty stage and the obligatory tumbleweed.

Rich looked down at his plate in horror: it was empty. 'What the hell have I just eaten?' he asked.

'I have no idea, except that you did it twice,' I replied, my thoughts in an absolute spin.

'Got to go to the bog,' he announced, clutching at his stomach.

We watched him lurch to the gents and then Caroline leant towards me.

'What did you say to her last night?' she demanded.

'I didn't say anything, she brought me round that script she'd been writing. It was really good and I said so.'

'Did she say anything else?'

'You mean anything else apart from the fact that she knew that I used to be of the Rich persuasion?'

'Yes.'

'Like what?'

'Like the fact that she just happens to be in love with you, you daft and ungrateful git.'

If it hadn't have been for the fact that Caroline had been my best friend since kindergarten I would have given her such a smack; as it was I just deflated visibly and sniffed. Please God don't let me blub in public it's so *Big Brother*.

'No, she didn't say anything at all about that.'

'Oh.'

'She kissed me.'

'Ah ... and?'

'I don't know.'

'Which is, I presume, the reason that you are sitting here with the sulks and she's resigned.'

'Possibly,' I admitted.

'Well?'

'Well what?'

'What are you going to do about it?'

'Shit Caroline, I don't really know. What the hell do you think I should do about it?'

We sat in silence until Rich returned. When he did I handed back the signed cheques and told him to go back to the office and let everyone know that Caroline and I would be out for the day.

He was, I think, going to try and stay to find out what was going on but both Caroline and I glared unblinkingly at him until he gave up and grudgingly went away.

After we were sure he had gone. Caroline got out her mobile and tried to contact Trudy. All she got was the busy signal from her landline and 'The caller is not available' from her mobile.

'You don't think that she'd do something silly, do you?' I asked.

'What – like cut her wrists in the bath or take an overdose?'

'Yes.'

'You may think you're good but you're not that good,' Caroline replied and then she had a bit of a rethink and grabbed her handbag, which had up to that point been providing an assault course-cum-booby trap for a steady stream of octogenarians. 'On the other hand she's emotionally disturbed ... '

'She's not that much of a fruit loop!' I exclaimed, with even to my own ears, surprising tones of defence.

'She must be to think that you're the best thing that happened to her since they legalised gay sex.'

'That's right, sink to my level.'

'Anyway I think we ought to just go and check just to make absolutely sure she's not going to take us to some tribunal for unfair dismissal.'

'What? Oh come on – she left us!'

'Yeah but why, eh? 'Cos you spurned her advances; that could be construed by some very sad and sick bastards as constructive dismissal.'

'What! Now look here ... I did nothing of the sort.'

'Alex, you and I both know that the law has nothing whatsoever to do with common sense or any notion of fair play.' And Caroline was up and heading towards the exit at an astonishing rate before I could even start to think of a suitable pithy reply.

I grabbed my things and ran after her, my heels click clacking on the polished stone floor.

'Will you wait for me!' I demanded, beginning to lose her. 'There is no way you should be running in your condition.'

She turned and fixed me with a patrician stare, her nostrils flaring.

'How the hell do you know?'

'Because I'm your best friend and I've known you since kindergarten,' I replied with a smile before adding, 'and you only eat chocolate dipped in tomato sauce when you're pregnant.'

Seventeen

When we finally got to Trudy's house, bickering all the way, it was almost three o'clock and hours and hours from when Trudy had arrived for her last day at the office.

I'd never actually been to her house before and was a bit surprised about how much it looked like a scaled-down version of mine. The garage was to one side and we stood next to the door and listened.

We couldn't hear anything, which was good news; she hadn't decided on asphyxiation by carbon monoxide, but it also meant that she may very well have already left.

We walked up to the front door and rang the bell. Then we listened, peered through the letterbox and then rang the doorbell again.

After awhile, net curtains started moving across the road and before someone called the police we sidled around to the side of the house, opened the little gate into the back garden and cautiously approached the back door. We banged on that as well and waited. Then we looked up. The bathroom window was open slightly and we exchanged a worried look.

'You don't think?' Caroline made slitting motions on her wrist with an imaginary knife and I went pale.

'No, I don't,' I said and ran to the conservatory which had been added on as a bit of an afterthought to the rear wall of the house by someone who should have had his building certificate confiscated and his arms and legs sawn off. The door was unlocked, so I pushed it open and raced in. Caroline arrived inside at the same time as me and we then both saw the pair of legs lying motionless on the floor in the lounge, the rest of the torso being hidden from view by a large, peach-coloured, squashy sofa.

We looked at each other and then both raced round to the other side and screamed. I mean we all screamed, even Trudy who was lying on the floor tapping into her laptop and oblivious to our presence because of the iPod earbuds in her ears.

I sat clutching my heart on one side of the sofa and Caroline sat clutching her tummy on the other whilst poor dear Trudy sat shaking in the middle.

'What the hell are you both doing here?' she asked.

'We thought you might ... '

'I might what?' she growled, her fright turning quickly to anger.

'Um.' I looked at Caroline and she looked at me as if to say you started this and I'm not helping you wriggle out of this one. 'I thought you might be doing something silly.'

'Silly? I'm actually sorting out that manuscript you liked, the one you said was good.'

'Ah, I did say it was good, didn't I?'

'It's why I resigned.'

I wracked my brains to see how one thing that I had said had led to her resignation and couldn't think of anything. 'Er?'

Trudy took a deep breath and glared at me. 'Don't you remember you said you couldn't really do both. Not work and write. You gave that lecture at the library last year.'

I must have looked suitably blank and stupid because Trudy screwed her eyes into two hard little slits and looked like she was just about to explode. 'The lecture about – you know – doing it all ... letting the brain work differently ... and what?'

'So it's nothing to do with ... with ... er?'

'You spurning my advances?'

'I didn't spurn them.'

'Well what *were* you doing?'

Caroline coughed and then got up and smoothed down her skirt. 'I'm going back to the office to make sure that idiot child Richard didn't lose half the cheques.'

I nodded and continued to stare at Trudy. I had never before really looked at her and she had really soft wavy hair and very, very, blue eyes. Violet even.

Trudy waited until she heard the click of the front door and turned her face towards mine.

'Look – I'm really sorry about last night – it was just a spur of the moment thing and Caroline – '

'Caroline?' I spluttered.

'Yeah, she said why not go for it.'

'Caroline – Caroline knows about you and about me and ... '

'Yes, you see it was really sort of her idea, get it out in the open, clear the air that sort of thing.'

I glared at the doorway, no wonder she had cleared off, the cow.

'Look I know that you didn't like it, the kiss I mean,' Trudy muttered, looking embarrassed and blushing furiously.

'I didn't say I didn't like it, I was just surprised.' I wanted to stroke her hair, I really wanted to give her a big hug and stroke her hair.

'So what do I do now?' she asked, suddenly no longer in the least bit terrible.

'Do it again.'

'What!'

'Just do it again.'

And she did, only this time I wasn't in the least bit surprised but after a while I think she was.

Eighteen

I called in sick the next day. Caroline answered the phone and demanded to see a certificate, so then I had to tell her I was still at Trudy's, only one floor above where she had left us.

'About bloody time,' Caroline snorted gleefully and then she hung up.

We spent the day experimenting with a variety of things Trudy had collected over the years, including a little PVC catsuit and some rather kinky-looking waders with diamante buckles. Another previously unused item was a strange looking wooden phallus she'd picked up whilst on a coach holiday in Germany. However the highpoint was quite possibly a pair of 'love eggs' from Scandinavia for which we had to change the batteries twice.

After that night the weekend stretched ahead and we decamped to my house, where my mother found us on Sunday morning sharing a bath, a bottle of champagne and our underwear.

'Oh good, you finally found a friend to play with,' she said in passing as she went down to the kitchen to prepare a celebratory tabasco and lemon cake.

The chap from the care home picked her up promptly at five and we then carefully cleaned the kitchen and threw everything we could find that had been newly cooked in the bin. I'd tried recycling my mother's culinary masterpieces by tipping them onto the bird table but as even the crows pushed the sandwiches over the edge, the dustbin was now the only option.

Monday came, I went back to work and hired a new managing assistant and Trudy embarked on her new career as writer and live-in lover.

Mother actually liked Trudy, which was a first as she'd never really taken to any of my other friends and associates including Caroline, whom she just about tolerated. Trudy however was greeted as the new messiah and we were regularly invited round to the home for tea. On the evening that mother finally passed away she kissed us both and palmed me a note which I read as we drove home in the rain little knowing that it was for the last time. The note, scrawled in my mother's almost illegible script, told me 'follow your heart instead of your head however strange the direction' and was signed 'as ever your loving if ill-advised mum'.

I sat in the darkened lounge after the call came from the home to say that she had passed away into that long goodnight and thought long and hard about life, the universe and everything and then went upstairs and had a long and frank chat with Trudy. The upshot of which is why I'm now standing in the porch of the registry office nervously awaiting Caroline to turn up with her better half, her kids and the rings.

We then delayed the honeymoon for a day or so until Trudy had finished the last page of her final proof and

Mother had been safely and quietly laid to rest. The only mourners were Caroline, Trudy, myself and the Vinnie Jones look alike and we all cried into our respective hankies as the coffin was laid into the family grave.

Then we swapped a hearse for a rather fast little Mercedes sports car and rattled off to a rather charming little hotel in Bournemouth which we found on the internet. I was absolutely determined to finally visit the New Forest and the Isle of Wight, something I had always wanted to do but for whatever reason had never done, and on the way we even acquired a tan, another thing I'd had on my personal wishlist for years.

We spent two happy and self-centred weeks exploring, eating and loving and then with a regretful sigh we packed up the car and drove back up to Little Comfrey and the real world.

When we finally arrived back at my house there were twenty-three messages from Caroline on the answer phone and they were all the same. 'Alex, it's Caroline, ring me when you get in.'

I frowned at the machine and then after glancing at the clock to see if it was too late to reasonably ring anyone picked up the phone and dialled her number. She picked up on the second ring, always a sure sign of trouble and I held my breath to see how bad it was.

'Caroline,' I said, 'you rang?'

'Oh thank God Alex, you're back.'

'Yes I am, indeed so, yes.'

'Alex, go and find a big bottle and a small glass and ring me back.'

'Really? It can't be that bad!'

'It's worse. Bottle, glass, ring me.' And she put the phone down on me.

I hastened off to do her bidding and then with the required objects in front of me and Trudy sitting perched on the easy chair opposite mine I rang Caroline back. This time she answered on the first ring.

'Alex I'm really, really sorry but ... '

'Come on Caroline, it can't possibly be that bad.'

'Your mother's will was read yesterday and she's left the firm to your Uncle Edwin ... '

'What!'

' ... and he refuses point blank to ever publish anything by that Abomination.'

'Abomination?'

'Trudy. He won't publish anything by her or by Wayne and Nigel. He's having all our writers vetted and if he disapproves of any of them, if there is even a sniff of anything sinful, be it adultery, greed, gluttony, anything, he's refusing to sign a contract or distribute their books.'

'But he can't do that!'

'Unfortunately he can and he has.'

'But ... '

'Alex, your mother made a new will and in it she left all the shares in the company to your Uncle Edwin. Nobody knows why, even the solicitor thinks it's odd but we have had the handwriting checked and apart from contesting the will there is nothing we can do.'

'Then we contest the will. Mother hated Uncle Edwin, wouldn't have him in the house, said all sorts of rude things about him and all the time.'

'To contest the will we need money and all the money ... '

'Is tied up in the firm.'

'Which you now don't own.'

'Shit.'

'I know at the time that going to your mother was the only way of baling us out because the bank wouldn't lend any more cash but ... '

'I know you did warn against it. The thing is, mother– '

'I know, but she wasn't well, was she?'

'And what about me? What does my wicked Uncle want to do about me?'

'He fired you yesterday, the day the shares passed on to him.'

I put the phone down as Caroline was still trying to apologise for something that wasn't her fault, and stared unseeingly at the floor.

That morning I went back to the office to collect my things before Uncle Edwin could stop me or change the locks. Caroline was in her room looking hormonal and very tearful and I walked towards her and gave her the biggest warmest hug that I could. After that I went round the office and embraced each and every employee that my Uncle hadn't fired. I promised to be back and then I walked away, a sob still ringing in my ears and I'm almost certain that it had come from Maria Coaltit.

I had to do something. I had to get my firm back. It was my business, my sweat, my blood and my tears and worth a cool million of anyone's money. What it would be worth after a month of my mad Uncle's ministrations I dreaded to think.

I drove slowly home, told a sombre Trudy that we were both out of work and then I went down to my allotment to dig up a few vegetables for tea and had a quiet cuppa in the potting shed and a long hard think.

A long hard think, about how to get away with the perfect murder.

Nineteen

I thought about ways of killing Uncle Edwin, I really did. I went through every crime book I had in the house, true or otherwise. I even resorted to watching re-runs of *Murder she Wrote* and *Poirot*.

I considered garrotting dear old Uncle Edwin with a bit of cheese wire, which was to my mind a perfect solution to the problem. Unfortunately I'd have ended up with having to do something with the body as there was no way that any one would be able to cut their own head off whilst simply sampling a hunk of old Cheddar cheese. I watched an old *Midsomer Murder* and did seriously consider taking his head off with a length of garden wire stretched across a bridleway but had no idea how I was going to get Uncle Edwin on a horse; the horse was apparently essential for the speed and height of the thing.

I seriously considered breaking into his house, stuffing sleeping tablets in his night-time cocoa and then holding a feather-filled pillow over his ugly wrinkled face until he stopped breathing. Unfortunately he had moved back into the old baronial pile and had not only employed a group of private security hoodlums but had wired the place inside and out as he was terrified of being burgled.

I then went through my book of poisons and couldn't find one that I could actually use with any degree of certainty. Uncle Edwin didn't drink, which made cyanide champagne a tad difficult. All the poisons I could find were either foul-tasting or bitter and as my dear sainted Uncle only drank water he would immediately twig that something was up. I seriously considered putting something in his food until I remembered how paranoid he was. A paranoia which had resulted in him buying a small terrier called Rupert who was given a small piece of each meal first. This also meant that my Uncle only ate food that was cold, which had resulted in him becoming a fruitarian and the dog a bag of unhappy bones.

I could pay someone to kill him, but as I'm technically still the heir I'm also the first person the police would haul in to assist them in their enquiries. Been there already, bought the t-shirt and definitely didn't ever want to have to do it again.

I couldn't do something to his car because he never drove himself and although I might loathe my only living relic I'd always rather liked Old Percy McIntosh who drove him around, even though he could hardly see and had the palsy.

I toyed with the idea of shooting him, running him down in a car – any car would do and I even thought long and hard about enticing him to the station and pushing him under a train. Any train.

There had to be a way of sending My Uncle Edwin to hell, I just couldn't find one that involved no direct contact and would work first time. What would I do with the body?

If there was no body the awful man could be declared dead after seven years. Unfortunately the way my Uncle was running the firm into the ground there would be absolutely nothing left to inherit in six months let alone six years.

I was still mulling over the possibility of a shooting accident on the glorious twelfth when the doorbell rang and shortly afterwards Wayne and Nigel were ushered in, still holding hands, into my study by a flour-coated Trudy. Cheese and leek flan, she mouthed by way of explanation and then shut the door and left us to it.

Wayne looked at Nigel and then Nigel looked at Wayne and then they both looked pleadingly at me.

'You have got to do something about that elderly odious homophobic relation of yours,' Wayne whined.

'He's utterly, utterly foul,' echoed Nigel. 'And an absolute philistine to boot!'

I pointed to the books littering every available surface and informed them that I was actually trying to do just that.

'Oh well,' Wayne said in a far perkier voice, 'in that case, please, please let us help you.'

They immediately fell upon my library of books and proceeded to trawl through the most interesting.

'Oh I love this one, I simply love it. *Why didn't they ask Evans?* by the divine Agatha. Don't you remember, Nigel? We watched it last week on Hallmark, the victim was stabbed with a dagger made of ice that the murderer kept concealed in a thermos flask. They only worked it out because of the tealeaf left in the wound. It was the perfect murder as the weapon melted.' Wayne rambled on until I had to inform him, rather reluctantly, as he was having so much fun imagining my Uncle gently congealing under a noonday sun, that firstly my Uncle never played golf and secondly that I seriously doubted that I could get close enough during daylight hours to administer the coupe de grace.

Undeterred, Nigel then discovered a website on his laptop devoted entirely to the making of explosive devices. Some of them did indeed look rather simple, so simple in fact that my Uncle would spot them within minutes, nor was he at all likely to travel by any form of public transport as he was scared witless of catching germs. He was by then as mad as a hatter, only marginally less amusing. Another reason why we decided to look elsewhere was that quite a few of the bombs looked dreadfully unstable, particularly the ones that you had to actually wear in some form or other. And then I remembered some TV series which had MI6 – or was it 5? – monitoring the websites such as the one Nigel was actually looking at just to see who was trying to get an Open University degree in anti-social behaviour.

After that we tried a couple of Rankin's, a Wingfield or two and discovered the *ABC Murders* under *The Good Thief's Guide to Vegas* and a well-thumbed copy of Donna Moore's *Old Dogs*. 'This is it!' Wayne gleefully cried, waving it in the air like an Olympic torch. We kill off a bunch of people using the A-Z and ensure that your Uncle Edwin is right slap bang in the middle. Nigel and I looked at each other, spotting the one and only flaw.

'Um Wayne sweetie, er ... the thing is, who else do we bump off?' Nigel tentatively asked.

'Oh bugger,' Wayne wailed, 'I'd not considered that.'

'Couldn't we blow up his house and blame the plumbing or the oven or something?' Nigel suggested, rubbing his hands together in desperation.

'Doesn't have any gas, just the electric,' I advised. 'And no, I don't think we can set fire to it either, or at least not in a way that doesn't shout arson the moment the fire inspectors get busy with their magnifying glasses and test kits.'

'We have to do something, our tea room depends upon it!' Nigel cried from the corner of the room where he was engrossed in a tattered and well-thumbed copy of *Woolly the Naughty Sheep*.

'Hang on a sec, what about your royalty cheque? I distinctly remember signing it,' I asked, looking up from a copy of *Strong Poison* by Dorothy Sayers.

'The old bastard cancelled all the cheques with your signature on, said that they were signed while he owned the company and that you had no authority. Had a hell of a row with the bank over it. Now he won't pay us because he says he refuses to support a couple of old fat Queens.'

'But he can't do that!'

'No, strictly speaking he can't and according to our lawyer he can be made to pay and the whole lot can be backdated but it will take months if not years to go to court, by which time we will have a legal bill roughly equalling the money we are attempting to get back and your darling little firm will already be firmly under the administrator's thumb or completely bankrupt.'

'Can't you contest your mothers will? I mean, everyone in the village knows that she was almost completely gaga,' Wayne asked not unreasonably.

'Same reason you don't want to sue for non-payment of royalties because by the time it gets to the Chancery court I won't have any estate left to claim.'

Wayne had by then finished *The Naughty Sheep* and was engrossed in Stuart MacBride's *Flesh House*. 'Couldn't we just eat him?' he asked.

Nigel and I exchanged a shocked look and both yelled a very firm 'No!' at the same time, then we sat and gloomily looked at the wealth of murderous material surrounding us, none of which was going to be of the slightest help.

They stayed for a slice of quiche and rocket salad, they even had a tranche of Trudy's lemon and cream sponge with homemade lemon curd. I offered them a really decent glass of Chablis as well but they both declined on the grounds that they were both depressed enough already and if they drank they dreaded what they might end up doing.

Trudy and I saw them to the door and then we both sat outside and finished up a couple of bottles of my best wine.

It was there that Albert and Mrs Coaltit found us, drinking Chablis and having a damn good weep.

Twenty

'Young Alex, you have got to do something about that bloody relative of yours, before I bean him over the back of the head with me best shovel,' Albert railed.

I looked at Albert with a certain amount of growing respect; a spade across the bald pate, why hadn't I thought of that? 'You'd really brain him?' I asked in a hopeful fashion. Yippee, problem solved and I would be able to honestly say, hand on heart that 'I was nowhere near the scene of the crime, officer'.

Maria looked at me and then at Albert and called us both silly old fools. I guessed that that option was out.

'Why what's he done now?' Trudy asked as she prised herself from her chair and wobbled off to the kitchen.

'Done! He's only gone and stopped my Maria's royalty cheque 'cos he said she was a red petticoated Jezebel, that's why,' Albert shouted.

Maria Coaltit nodded, although she actually looked a little pleased by the biblical reference.

'Said she was no better that she should be and that he was going to tell the wife, and good luck on that one considering she's been having it off up the allotments with that bleeding Sam Parish. Bloody years that's been going on.'

'Why don't you kick her out?' I asked.

'Cos it's her bleedin house ain't it, her old dad left it to her and then to the kids after, and where would I live?'

'Well in that case why don't you leave and er ... ' I looked rather pointedly at Maria and then back at the gently simmering Albert.

'Oh I couldn't do that, what live in sin and Maria the Postmistress and all. What would people think? Couldn't hold me head up during communion let alone the family service if I did that.'

At that point Trudy returned from the kitchen with two further wine glasses and a fresh bottle of wine.

'You don't have any beer, do you love? Only wine gives me wind,' Albert pointed out before adding in apologetic tones that he was sure it was very nice wine for all that.

I sighed and in not an entirely sober fashion stood up, swayed to the back door, entered the kitchen, located the fridge and after a few minutes reappeared with a couple of bottles of Highlander. Trudy hastily took them from me as I swayed uncertainly and Albert gratefully poured the majority of his bottle into a large balloon glass, Maria having already made impressive inroads into the Chablis.

We sat in silence as the sun slipped behind the trees at the end of my garden and the birds hiding amongst the trees and shrubs started up a chorus worthy of a West End production of *Les Miserables*. Then much to everyone's astonishment Maria had a sip of her third refill and burst into tears.

'What on earth is wrong, Mrs Coaltit?' I asked.

'It's nothing, it's just that that awful, horrid, foul, nasty little man sent me a letter and I have to quit the post office,' she sobbed. 'And I've lived there ever since I was born when my parents moved us all up from Wigan.'

'He's done what?' Albert roared. 'He's got no fuckin' right to do that!'

'Well actually he has,' I murmured. 'Mother still owned the deeds to most of the village houses except for the vicarage, church, church hall and the school. Although I suppose for a long time we owned even them.'

Trudy looked at me in a shocked fashion. 'Alex – just exactly how much does your family own?'

'Most of the village, the retirement home ... actually that was mother's idea as she didn't want to live on her own and liked a bit of company, some real estate in the city, my firm to stop the bank foreclosing and about five hundred acres of prime grouse shooting country up near Inverness. I think that there is also an old and dilapidated tower house on the West coast somewhere as well.'

'Right, well in that case we have to call a village meeting before it's too late.'

And with that she stormed off to the kitchen for the telephone. Suddenly sober I followed her, closely escorted by Albert and his paramour; she was absolutely right – it wasn't just the firm that would die with all my writers sobbing in their garrets but the village itself and although I wasn't the ideal heir, I was still a Moncreiff and a Moncreiff of Little Comfrey to boot.

Twenty-One

The four of us spent almost three hours ringing round and eventually everyone we had rung, with the exception of Albert's wife, agreed to meet in the church hall the following night at seven o'clock sharp.

To be honest I thought that if we were lucky about a quarter would turn up and so it was with some surprise that I saw that everyone had made it. Including Albert's estranged spouse, who sat right at the front with a grey-headed old codger carrying a stick, who I presumed was the infamous Sam Parish.

Albert and Maria were there, as were young Jasmine and Tony the chef still in his work clothes of black and white checked trousers, white jacket and black bandana. Old Clarkson our resident cabby had turned up with young Clarkson who had bottle glasses and a decided lisp. The stationmaster was there with young Brian, who had brought a pair of secateurs just to be on the safe side, or so he informed me. The law was represented by our local bobby who was telling everyone that he wasn't moving from his nice new house to that grotty little 1950s shitehole for anyone, even if Uncle Edwin did know the soddin' Chief

Constable. Even the church was represented by our local vicar and his wife. All my writers were there and every member of staff including Caroline, who had that day been fired for having the temerity to ring me. There was also a smattering of strangers and one lone reporter who had got the date wrong and was expecting to talk to and photograph the new batch of Brownies.

We were just about to start when the door flew open and Uncle Edwin appeared in a gust of wind and a small vortex of autumn leaves. It was quite an entrance and every conversation was instantly terminated as he stalked to the front, his old greatcoat flapping around him and a smell of mothballs shadowing his every move.

Trailing behind him was the Vinnie Jones look-alike from the nursing home and Old Percy the chauffeur.

'Stand down young Alexander, I have the floor,' he hissed.

As a body every beady eye fastened on me.

'Oh didn't he tell you, I'm sorry didn't *she* tell you? Not shy are you lad? Want to know what your sainted Marguerite Moncreiff did with part of the Moncreiff inheritance? She paid, nay wasted, good money on changing her son and heir Alexander Neville Moncreiff into that!'

I stared at him and in that instance could have torn off my own arm and beaten him to death with the soggy end. He must have sensed something because he curled his lip and then turned on Trudy.

'You see he isn't a dyke after all girlie, he's a man, one of them, so what do you think of that, eh?'

Trudy looked at me and then stood as straight as she could and glared at him with tears in her eyes.

'I don't give a rat's arse who Alex is or was, because the person inside is the one I will always love regardless of gender.' And then she gave him the best right hook I've ever had the privilege to witness.

Uncle Edwin backed away, blood pouring from his nostrils.

'You bluddy whore ... you bloke dy dose.'

'Good! I wish I'd broken your bloody head.'

'You go girl!' Wayne and Nigel shouted from the back.

'Blofficer arrest that harblot,' my Uncle stuttered, beside himself with rage.

Constable Macleod sat down on his seat and looked about him. 'What Harblot? I see no harblot? Anybody here see a harblot?' There was complete silence broken by Constable Macleod folding his arms across his chest and announcing to the ceiling that he hadn't seen anything and that the poor old sod must have had one drink too many and fallen down the stairs.

Slowly Old Percy Parish moved to the front, his hands shaking. He was assisted by the Vinnie Jones look-alike. Uncle Edwin, still dripping blood from his nose, moved a step towards him and muttered.

'You saw it Percy didn't you? that harblot bloke dy dose.'

'Aye I saw it and I can see why the Missus set such store by her, you may be the squire now but you ain't no gentleman like Mistress Alex and her dad before her and you can drive yer own bleedin' car. I quit. Come along son, I can feel one of me moments comin' on.'

Uncle Edwin went puce and raised a fist, he even managed one step towards old Percy before Percy's lad turned on him.

'You lay one finger on my old man and they'll have difficulty in finding enough bits to fit in a matchbox.' And he said it with such quiet menace that we all backed off, leaving a little well of space around him and Edwin.

'And if he don't do it, I'll nail your balls to the walls for losing me my job in the bank and don't think I won't.' Colin yelled from the back as he waved a bright red staple-gun in the air.

And then someone started a slow handclap, and someone else joined in and shouted '*Out, Out, Out.*' Other people picked the chant up including the vicar and then the foot stamping started. Uncle looked at me with such hatred in his eyes that I took a hasty step back. He then turned and limped away, holding a large cotton handkerchief under his nose. Slowly he negotiated the steps that led off the stage and then threaded his way through the standing crowd of ill-wishers and out of the main door. By the time he reached the door I seriously wondered if he was going to be lynched, which he might have been if Constable Macleod hadn't have given him a police escort to the door. The crowd suddenly went quiet as he turned and tried to thank his protector.

'Don't thank me, I was only doing my job, the job of protecting that lot against themselves. But I come off duty in five minutes time so who knows what might happen then.'

My Uncle looked at the crowd glaring at him from inside the hall and at the young policeman glaring at him from outside and made a dash for his car. It was only when he was inside that he realised he had no keys. I picked them up from where Percy had thrown them and walked down the aisle and out into the autumnal air. Uncle sat bolt upright inside his elderly Bentley, the sweat dripping from his brow.

I tapped on the window and waggled them at him, then I dropped them on the bonnet and sauntered off to the pub, closely followed by the entire meeting.

As soon as we had gone Uncle opened the door, looked about him very carefully and crawled on all fours until he found the keys in the gutter, clambered back inside, started the car after the third attempt and then roared backwards into a streetlamp. He then crashed the gears around until he shot forwards into the parish noticeboard. After that he proceeded to drive the car up and over the kerb, knocking over four wheelie bins, seven dwarfs, a miniature wishing well and a rather grand display of late flowering roses. Eventually he got back onto the road and drove on the wrong side of it until he hit the roundabout. Which he did quite literally. He then mounted the kerb again, drove over the newly replanted flower clock and then careered off down the road as he headed for the family manor house. And how do I know this? One of the local hoodies, quite a nice lad called Patrick who did the paper round every weekend instead of his older brother, who was normally unfit to do anything on a Saturday morning on account of his passion for sniffing anything in an aerosol or a tube, had filmed the entire thing on his mobile phone. He then posted it on YouTube and it was then downloaded and played on a loop for the entire village to enjoy on the local publicans widescreen television, imported especially for the Six Nations rugby.

Everyone cheered as we watched the entire thing again, especially the bit where Uncle Edwin crawled back into his car after grabbing the car keys. Constable Macleod was particularly happy and he even whistled as he also had video evidence in order to write out the correct number of summonses for all the traffic violations. He was almost ecstatic when I told him that to my certain knowledge dear old Uncle Edwin held no valid driving licence, in fact I doubted very much if he had ever passed his test.

Twenty-Two

It was with slightly more of a spring in my step, albeit a very wobbly one, that I proceeded back to my house later that same evening. Trudy had fallen asleep in the snug and as she looked so peaceful and was so very popular that I let sleeping dogs lie and decided to go for a bit of an amble before attempting the stairs to Bedfordshire. I was halfway to poking the key in the door when a steady hand extracted it from my wavering paw and I was carefully manhandled inside. The door was closed behind me, again very carefully and then the dark figure went around closing all the curtains, while I stood propped up beside the front door against the elephant's foot umbrella stand. After a while the intruder tiptoed back to me and, steering me by my elbows, negotiated us both into the kitchen. All the blinds were down and all the curtains carefully closed so that not a solitary chink of light could escape. The lights were suddenly snapped on blindingly and I came face to face with the Vinnie Jones impersonator, Percy's son.

'Look,' I said, 'I have no idea what you want but I can't keep calling you Vinnie even if it is just inside my head.'

He grinned at that and openly laughed. A laugh which happily rumbled around the room like a released buffalo on Red Bull. 'But you can, mate, as the names Vincent after the painter but everyone calls me Vinnie.'

'Okay.'

'So, got any decent coffee?' he asked, looking around my kitchen with interest. 'That Fairtrade Brazilian will do.'

'Um I may have some somewhere?' I replied, digging about in the cupboards. Finally I extracted the cafetiere from the dishwasher, found a packet of ground coffee which was of a suitable brand and blend and put the kettle on.

'Are you sober Alex?'

'Yes Vinnie I am almost sober and getting soberer every minute.'

'Good, 'cos I need you sober with all them little clever grey cells of yours up and running.'

'Why?'

'You and me, Alex, is going to break into your uncle's house the moment he's arrested for dangerous driving, driving without a licence, endangerment, reckless whatsit and driving over a roundabout. There may be a few minor infringements for damaging council property, failing to stop at the scene of an accident and so on and so forth.'

'There was the mention of not stopping at a junction and driving without lights as well.'

'I'd forgotten about them.'

'Do you think our local sheriff will be able to make the gnome-killing stick?'

'Let's not be greedy.'

'No I suppose not, still, it would good look in the papers. *Gnome murderer runs amok amongst the sleepy village of ...* '

Vinnie made the coffee and then handed me a cup of what could at best be described as rocket fuel. I took a sip and then another. It tasted like I'd imagined creosote would taste but it was indeed slowing down the rate at which the room was continuing to turn whenever I was stupid enough to close my eyes.

'Vinnie.'

'Yes, Alex.'

'Just why are we talking about breaking into my wicked uncle's house?'

'Cos your old mum was bloody good to me, that's why.'

'Right, and that makes so much sense.'

I took another sip of coffee and then lurched to the fridge to see if there was either anything with a lot of protein in it or vitamin C. I found a packet of sliced roast beef and a carton of orange juice. It was a matter of moments to open both and then I sat back down on a kitchen stool and after offering them to Vinnie, who shook his head, pigged the lot.

'And just how do you reckon we are going to get in?' I asked through a mouthful of red meat.

'I have a few tools and er ... tricks of the trade so to speak, on account of having visited many of Her Majesty's Prisons.'

'Oh.'

Vinnie laughed at the shocked look on my face and poured us both another rich steaming cup of coffee.

'It's not what you think. I was a prison warder for a few years and then an inspector. Met a lot of blokes inside, some of 'em were good enough blokes if you didn't wind 'em up. Some even showed me a few tricks of the trade on account of feeling sorry for me.'

'Sorry ... ?'

'I was forever losing my house keys, and her indoors could nag for bloody England so the lads showed me how to get in after she'd locked me out.'

I blinked as I'd always thought that Percy didn't have any daughters-in-law or at least he never mentioned any, and down at The Old Beagle he was known for miles around as the biggest talker this side of the Tweed. 'What happened to her?' I asked, nearly burning my mouth on the almost super-heated fluid.

'Nothing, we just grew apart, couldn't have any kids – not her fault nor mine, just one of them things, but she was that desperate and we tried everything, in the end she just left, went off to live with her sister in Oz.'

'Oh.'

'Turned out to be good timing really, as Dad wasn't none too clever by then, so I went to work at your mum's place. Much the same job as prison really, keeping them all in and dragging 'em back when they went AWOL or forgot that they were living there at all.'

'Well that makes more sense than some reasons I've heard.'

'I bet.' Vinnie grinned at me and poured himself more coffee. 'Want any more?' he asked, waving the cafetiere around.

'No thanks, I've plenty.'

'I liked your old mum, she was a real lady. And before she died she asked me to do a special job for her.'

'Oh?'

'Yeah, she wanted me to find out what happened to your dad.'

I nearly choked on the dregs of my coffee. 'But he left ran off with the games mistress from the convent school in Much Barking, everyone knew about it!' I exclaimed.

'Oh yeah, everyone all right, everyone knew including your mum.'

'Well?'

'Your dad got about a bit, so your mum told me, couldn't keep it in his trousers and your mum let him because they'd married with an understanding.'

'What kind of understanding?'

'You ever heard of the Bluebell Girls?'

'Well, yes, of course, everyone has.'

'Your dear old mum was one of them girls, posh stripper is what my dad called her and she knew it. What's more so did your dad's family and it didn't go down well in certain parts, especially not with brother Edwin. But your dad wanted to get married and have kids, in particular a son.'

I sighed and looked down into my mug.

'Your mum married for money and a home, same as most did then and your dad married to keep his brother out of the family trough 'cos even then he was a really nasty piece of work. Interested now, eh? Thought you might be. Then your mum gives birth to you and no one knows what to do. So they say it's a boy just to keep your wicked uncle at bay and then they starts trying for another one. Way I heard it as soon as they had another boy they was going to let you grow up as a girl cos by then that's what they reckoned you was.'

So that's why mother paid for everything. I'd wondered at the time but she never said and I'd never asked.

'Yep nothing stronger than maternal guilt, apart that is for maternal love and the poor old lady had plenty of that.'

Vinnie gave me a sideways look to see how I was taking it before dropping his final verbal bombshell.

'Only before they can try again and while you is still looking like a stuffed sprout your dad ups and leaves, supposedly with the young woman from up at the school.'

'But ... '

'Your dad would never have left your mum like that, or you for that matter – according to my mum and dad he took you everywhere and when no one was around he used to dress you up in a long pink frock and call you his little Alexandra, his little princess. Unfortunately your bleedin' Uncle saw you both one day down by the stream and even though your dad pretended to be drunk I don't reckon your evil Uncle Edwin believed him at all.'

'Oh. So?'

'Your mum had me track that schoolteacher down and I did ... she told me that your dad was supposed to meet her for a bit of hanky panky in the old foreman's cabin down by the gravel pit only he never turned up. Your uncle did though, made her an offer she couldn't refuse and told her a few tales out of school. Like the fact that your dad was having a laugh at her expense and so was the school and said how saddened he was by the whole thing and how he would compensate her for her loss of reputation and gave her a ticket to Canada and a reference for a job over there.'

'The bastard!'

'Thought you'd see it that way, your mum certainly did and told me to follow it up as far as I could.'

'So you went to Canada?'

'No, Cardiff. She didn't want to bugger off to Canada so she went home to her mum and dad. She did write to your mum and dad though but they never got the letters. I tracked her down through that Friends Reunited site. She told me everything, I told your mum and the next thing I know your old mum is found wandering around the old pit in her nightie, catches pneumonia and dies. Then suddenly this will appears. Now I know your old mum and she would never ever have signed anything like that. But that bastard brother-in-law of hers would and could. You know what he got sent down from Oxford for?'

'No, do tell.'

'Forging cheques, common or garden fraud. Family hushed it up, sent him off to live in South Africa for a bit with some distant cousin.'

'But, but that would mean that he could well have murdered my mother!'

'Oh yes indeed he could and I believe and so does my old dad, that he murdered your old man as well.'

I sat in the manner of a stunned fish and felt angry tears pricking at the corners of my eyes and then I had a single solitary horrible thought.

Oh my God it was hereditary!

Vinnie turned and grinned at me and then banged his empty cup down on the kitchen table.

'And that is why you and me is going to break into his house and find something, anything, that can prove any or all of what I've just told you.'

I shook my head as a puzzled thought shot through my quickly sobering brain. 'But why would my mother go down to the old gravel works in the first place?'

'This is a guess and only a guess mind, but I reckon she found something that proved that that was where your dad was murdered, in fact he may for all we know still be there.'

'Why the hell didn't she just come to me, why after all this time did she have to go all secret squirrel?'

Vinnie shrugged and then stood up.

'So, you coming or what?' He asked.

'Oh yes I'm coming all right, wild horses couldn't stop me.'

Twenty-Three

We crouched at the side of the main gates and waited. A dog barked in the distance and was then answered by at least two more. There was a short silence and then the distant barking started up again. A large and rather scruffy dog of the Old English Sheepdog variety ambled past accompanied by a smaller, even scruffier hound of at least fifty-seven varieties and disappeared around a corner of the lane. I had a fleetingly surreal moment of wondering whether I had strayed into a rerun of *One Hundred and One Dalmatians*, reinforced by my companion's whisper that wasn't there a cat as well?

I shrugged as I couldn't actually remember.

Nothing else happened for a bit, so we sat with our backs to a large and towering beech tree and ate a bar of chocolate and then I cleaned my nails with a toothpick I'd drunkenly picked up at some restaurant and stashed in my pocket. I say drunkenly because I couldn't remember either doing it or why I would even want to.

I had moved on to the other hand when Vinnie shushed me and we hastily bit the dust, or rather the leaf mould and bracken surrounding our hiding place. A car, not my uncle's Bentley which was strangely enough in for minor repairs of the bonnet, wings – both sides – and the boot, went sedately past us. The driver was new but the figure in the back wasn't. My uncle was sitting ramrod straight and appeared to be hitting his head on the roof at regular intervals, he also appeared to be shouting but whether at the driver or his phone I wasn't too sure, nor, to be frank, did I care.

'Come on, move your arse, Alex,' Vinnie hissed and we ran, still half-crouching, to the gates and slipped between them before they closed. To be honest I had never understood the point of paying a small or even medium-sized fortune of hard-earned cash or even misappropriated funds for state of the art security and then installing a bloody great gold embellished gate, which then took at least three minutes to close. Unless, of course, you had a guard with a Kalashnikov waiting at the side until it did close. For the sake of our current mission it was just as well that my wicked uncle hadn't actually cottoned on to this potential breach in security. Although to be fair to the old sod he probably had, he was just a bit of a snob and liked big expensive in-your-face ironmongery to keep the riff raff impressed. Besides which he was far too tightfisted to pay any extra salary bills, so instead he relied on technology. Thinking of which led me to look up at the camera suspended from a pole above the left hand gate post, and another blinked at us, its red light glowing, from above a bracket nailed onto a tall and balding elm. Vinnie produced a large sheet of silver foil and handed me an identical square.

'Alex,' he hissed, 'hold this out in front of you particularly over your face and then walk at a crouch until we get out of range.'

It was a clever trick and one which I had never ever thought of but would definitely use in my next book if I ever wrote one. I realised, as we hit the drive and stood up, that whoever looked at the tapes afterwards would see reflections of trees and leaves at around waist height but nothing useful with which to identify us, as we were both wearing dark trousers and black plimsolls, the type sold in their millions to schoolkids everywhere.

We didn't come across any more cameras until we got around to the back of the house, where we played the selfsame trick until Vinnie got the old door to the coal hole opened. We slid down into the blackened maul, now bereft of coal but filled with logs, and scrabbled our way towards the entrance to the cellar. Vinnie switched his torch on and played it around the walls to ensure that my uncle hadn't decided to splash out on any other security equipment that he didn't know about. Then we slid silently to the door that separated the cellar from the steps that led up to the cupboard under the main stairs. Vinnie produced a set of keys and unlocked the door. We waited just in case it had been alarmed and then we moved forwards, this time slowly and very carefully. Then I held the big torch whilst Vinnie produced a set of wire cutters and some metal electrical clips, the kind you get at school to use in physics experiments involving alternating and direct currents, and proceeded to deal with the security. It was all there in neat little plastic boxes, all carefully labelled so that even the G4 man knew what he was doing when he came out to test the system. My mother had had it installed originally when she'd turned the place into a care home of sorts and because she didn't want unsightly boxes and wires ruining the nineteenth-century wallpaper had had the lot carefully stuck in the cupboard under the stairs. She was always one for things being out of sight, out of mind even before the onset of old age and her mistaken belief that she was the Little Comfrey equivalent of Gary Rhodes, whom she adored.

Vinnie went about the business of disabling the system in his usual careful and cautious way as if born to play the part of Jeeves to my Wooster, while I stood in a corner and held the torch steady.

After about ten minutes he'd finally cut the last wire and made the last bridge between various sections. I'd asked as he'd started to snip away, why we didn't just switch the light on, to which he'd answered that my clever bastard of an uncle had connected the light switch directly to a panic button line and unless you knew the security number to disable it first, we'd be knee-deep in members of the constabulary before we could say 'Oh shit, what's that bloody awful noise.'

After Vinnie had stowed away his equipment in what looked suspiciously like Caroline's last rather expensive make-up bag, complete with the little Velcro pouches for brushes, files and nail scissors we quietly opened the door and slipped catlike into the hall.

Stealthily we padded across the garishly carpeted floor, the carpet picked during my mother's brief fling with Carnaby Street and magic mushrooms, and stopped at the door to the library.

'Why here?' I asked Vinnie.

'Cos,' Vinnie replied as he began trying out keys, 'I've managed to check all the others including his bedroom, the ensuite, the attic, the kitchens , storerooms garage and cellars ... I even braved the roof and the old stable block. This room, however, I could never enter unless your bleedin' uncle was actually in it, sitting in that black leather chair of his and doing his James Bond villain impression. Bastard needs to get a cat to do it properly.'

He paused. There was silence, followed by a click and we were in, Charlie Howard and Raffles would have been proud.

The library was actually bigger, darker and more full of books than I remembered. In fact there were books everywhere you looked, on shelves, on tables, the large desk at the window, the Edwardian club chairs either side of the fireplace and in piles all over the floor.

'Good grief!' I exclaimed 'I'd never, ever considered my Uncle a prolific reader.'

Then I took a closer look and a lot of them appeared to be mine.

Vinnie whistled as he picked one up and looked first at the title and then at the garish cover.

'Cats and condoms?' he muttered. 'Interesting – and it's one of yours too.'

'One of my first, not particularly good and only sold about a hundred, besides which the publisher was about as much good as a chocolate teapot.'

'And this?' Vinnie asked holding up one which had a clothes line full of very frilly knickers and one butchers knife.

'Actually that wasn't bad, and its now in its third or fourth reprint, still get a nice fat royalty cheque every third Tuesday in March.'

'So you was a writer.'

'I still am, just don't have time to do much.'

'When this is over, you need to get away, find somewhere nice and quiet and write the next Booker.'

'I might at that,' I agreed and sighed. 'Although I'd rather win a CWA dagger or some chain store award for the best new fiction.'

'Why?'

'You sell more, bigger royalty cheques and you don't turn into a pompous git overnight ... or as much as one.'

Vinnie began tapping the wooden panels between the bookshelves and I watched him in mute fascination, until curiosity got the better of me and I asked him what the hell he was up to.

'There's a safe in here somewhere between that Old Master and the window. I'm just not sure where the bastard keeps it. You check the desk to see if you can find anything interesting, he leaves the keys taped underneath.'

I went over to the large oak and leather-topped antique and searched around with my fingers until I found them. Carefully I went through each and every drawer until I came across a sheath of paper which looked oddly familiar.

Vinnie whistled and then as I looked up from my search a panel sprung sideways revealing an old antiquarian safe. Vinnie got it open in record time and I shut the drawer I had been looking in, carefully locked it as I had done all the others I'd opened, and then stuck the keys back in their hiding place. Vinnie, wearing a pair of catering gloves, moved slowly and lightly from one thing to another showing me each item as he went. One of them was my mother's original will, the one that mentioned the fact that my Uncle could go to hell in a handbasket and she'd be happy to watch him burn.

'Why on earth would he still keep it?' Vinnie asked, waving the pages about.

'Maybe to prove that his was written afterwards, perhaps he needed to forge the witnesses' signatures.' I shrugged and ran tired fingers through my hair.

'Witnesses?'

'Witnesses, you know the ones that witnessed the original will, the elderly retainers who had all over the last month or so gone to meet the great employer in the sky. Just a minute, how convenient is that!' I wracked my brains to think how they had met their individual ends and nothing stood out as extraordinary; he was really quite a clever bastard when you thought about it.

Then Vinnie found a box. A black velvet box. He opened it and we both gazed upon a large gold signet ring with the initials RCM engraved on the black onyx in the centre.

I'd seen something similar before and then I looked up at the painting of my great-grandfather Richard Cuthbert Moncreiff the third and I felt a frisson of electricity run down my spine.

'Well?' Vinnie asked. 'You've gone as pale and sickly looking as mum's pastry.'

'He keeps trophies.'

'Who?'

'Uncle Edwin, the will isn't because he needs it, it's because he wants to take it out and gloat!'

'Ah.'

'Look,' I said, and pointed up at the folded hands in the painting above the fireplace. On one of the podgy fingers a large ring could be seen, the selfsame ring that he held in his hands.

'So it was some old bloke's?' Vinnie shrugged.

'Listen Vinnie, this could be really important. That ring is always handed down upon death to the next in line and the last person to wear it was my father. He never ever took it off.'

Vinnie and I looked at it.

'He never took it off?' Vinnie repeated thoughtfully. 'How do you know he didn't stick it on the side of the bath or summat and your uncle didn't just pick it up and keep it?'

'Because my father inherited it when he was in his late teens and was bean-pole thin. By the time he married my mum he'd thickened out and he couldn't get it off even if he'd tried. Mum said she'd begged him to go to the jewellers and have it cut off and made wider but dad wouldn't hear of it.'

'So.'

'So, the only way to get this ring off would have been to have cut it off. That or kidnap him, stuff him in a small room and starve him until it came off naturally.'

'Bit *Silence of the Lambs* that, Alex.' Vinnie looked around in a pointed fashion and I had to admit that it definitely wouldn't have been to my uncle's rather conservative taste.

Vinnie took the ring out and with a thin pencil torch looked at it and whistled. Then he beckoned me over and we looked at it again with the large magnifying glass my uncle kept on his desk next to an alabaster bust of William Shakespeare. Carefully we turned it under the light and gasped simultaneously as we saw the tiny brown spots clinging to the hallmark inside.

'Obviously didn't manage to clean it completely after all,' Vinnie stated. 'And forty years on I bet some boffin can get a DNA match.'

'But to do that we have to have a body to match it with.'

'Yeah well, I have an idea about that and I may even have a plan.' And so saying, Vinnie put the ring back in the box and then carefully placed the box exactly where he had found it. Then he closed the safe door, twiddled the knob back to where it had been and re-closed the panel.

'But?' I queried, 'why leave the evidence?'

'Cos if we take it there is no evidence, or at least not enough to convince the police that your uncle did murder your parents.'

Vinnie had a very valid point and so we checked the room to ensure it was exactly as we'd left it and then we went back to the cupboard under the stairs, after very carefully relocking the library door.

Inside Vinnie slowly and methodically removed the clips, leaving just the snipped wires, went back out into the hall, unlocked the front door and then leaving me on the doorstep went back in and switched on the understairs light. The alarm filled the still of the night and with matching grins we scampered back to the gate and hid in the shadows until the local constabulary roared up, closely followed by my uncle who was the only one who had the remote control to open the gate. We waited until they had raced past us and then we sidled around the gate, which was still very slowly closing and vanished into the surrounding woodland.

I thanked Vinnie as we parted company at the war memorial and sauntered home deep in thought.

I'd seen that manuscript I'd found not long ago and he'd even kept my carefully worded rejection slip. No wonder he'd asked for it to be sent back to a post office box number. I frowned in concentration as I remembered my mother making scathing allusions to her brother-in-law's dyslexia and her complete puzzlement as to how he'd managed to get into Oxford.

And then it hit me, just how real were his 'reasons to kill'?

And now I began to understand just why he'd come after me and mine.

He was a rejected writer and had been for some time, judging by the pile of slips and letters under my own. He was out for revenge, pure and simple, and unfortunately for me he didn't have the means to bankrupt any of the other publishers he'd sent his wretched manuscript to.

And now that he had his own publishing firm and with all my marketing department's skills he could get a copy of his demented and badly written screwball of a book onto any bookshelf in any bookstore in the country. What he couldn't do was to get anyone to read it.

Which maybe I could use, maybe just maybe I could twist the knife in just long enough for him to lose that legendary cool, enough time for me to avenge not only my parents but all the others he'd helped move on to that great big waiting room in the sky.

Twenty-Four

Vinnie phoned at almost the same time as I arrived home.

'This cunning plan of mine,' he whispered. 'I've had a bit of a think and we need to talk to a few people about it.'

'A few people?'

'No more than necessary, just people who want to get even, those the old bastard's upset in some way.'

'That's half the bloody village, Vinnie.'

'Yeah I know, and that's why fat Clarry says we can have the back room at the pub. Meet you there in about half an hour and bring some dosh, 'cos it's your round first.'

The back room at the local hostelry was, when I eventually got there, packed to the gunwales, even Colin turned up still clutching his stapler. Vinnie had stuck a big map of the village and the surrounding area on the wall and had started up a kitty for the drinks. Asking me to fork out the first round was, he admitted, his idea of a joke.

No wonder he made a good screw.

Something I was very glad I hadn't repeated out loud as Trudy may have taken it the wrong way, and the rest of them definitely would.

Tony the Chef was there with Jasmine at his side and little Tony who was beginning to show under her waistband. This was probably the reason why she had recently stopped wearing skimpy little cropped tops for rather more comfortable and longer smocks.

Colin handed round the drinks, showing everyone who evinced any interest at all just exactly how good his stapler was. After he managed to staple his finger to a beer mat we took it away from him and fat Clarry locked it up under the bar until closing time.

Percy beamed at everyone and recanted between almost ladylike sips of his beer a blow-by-blow account of his telling Edwin Moncreiff just what he could do with his job and where he could stick his contract of employment. He was also going to tell the entire village about my uncle's penchant for fluffy slippers with rabbit's ears on the side. Something that he apparently had hidden in his wardrobe together with two riding whips and an inflatable bonking sheep.

Vinnie and I exchanged identical looks of disbelief, then Vinnie had a quiet word with his dad who went very pale, looked at me, swallowed and then went and sat in the corner next to Albert and Sam Parish. Sam and Albert had obviously made up as it had been Sam's gnomes that the wicked squire had mown down and Albert's carefully replanted roundabout that he'd driven over.

In fact the entire village had turned out with the exception of the Vicar, who had sent his apologies but he'd had the Little Acorns and the wardens to sort out, and Constable Macleod who was still up at the big house sorting out the burglar alarm.

After we had all settled down Vinnie produced a whistle and blew upon it. Silence descended in a suddenness that was almost louder than the actual noise that had preceded it.

We all sat and watched in abject fascination as he turned to his map and pointed to my childhood home the old manor house.

'Right then you 'orrible lot, this is where public enemy number one lives.'

'I thought Mr Edwin lived there?' Big Tony's mum loudly whispered in a voice the querulous pitch of which could have carried it to the Orkneys.

'He does,' Big Tony stated.

'But ... '

'Mum.'

'What?'

'Shut up!'

Vinnie rolled his eyes heavenwards and then glared at the pair of them. Big Tony and his mum both blushed bright scarlet and after a suitably dramatic pause Vinnie started again.

'Or Mr Edwin Moncreiff as he is otherwise known.'

'Or that mad bastard,' Albert interjected. We all looked at him and his Jason who promptly and very quietly also told his belligerent parent to shut the fuck up before Vinnie lived up to his namesake and went off to find a sawn-off. Albert went pale, gave Vinnie a frightened glance and then muttered 'Sorry pal'.

Vinnie sighed and tried to start again.

'Right then, he – Edwin Moncreiff alias public enemy number one alias the mad bastard – lives here. And we need him to go here.' On the second here he pointed to the old quarry workings and everyone but me looked a little puzzled.

'And before your mum says anything Tony none of you need to know why.'

The frowns cleared up and they all looked happy again.

'You see I had a bit of a think and – if we do all want to get rid of him?'

There was a collective 'Yes'.

'Then the best way is to all do it and to do that we all need to be at the quarry with one of these.'

He held up a homemade catapult, which consisted of a thin bit of branch which ended in a V shape, a piece of thick elastic tied to each of the prongs and a small piece of leather sewn onto the elastic in the middle.

'You will also need a small stone from the quarry.'

Again there was a collective look of bafflement.

'Once he has been lured to the quarry we all let rip with our stones and one of them should be enough to knock him out, especially if you all aim for the head. That way no one knows which one actually killed him.'

It was brilliant, I thought, absolutely brilliant except for one slight flaw.

'What if ... ' I stammered, 'what if he doesn't actually, um,you know, die?'

'Well if we stone him for long enough he's bound to collapse at some point, then we can drag him to the water in the middle and hold him there until he drowns.'

'Oh.'

'And another thing ... Alex you are going to have to leave the village, go somewhere with lots of people and stay out until he's dead, because as next of kin the police will investigate you first.'

I looked around at all my new found friends, they were all nodding and smiling and delighted to be doing me a big favour in getting rid of my last surviving relative.

'Just where did you get the idea for all of this from?' I asked in as casual a manner as I could.

'From here, from Dame Agatha, the greatest ever exponent of the whodunnit.' And he waved a copy of *Murder on the Orient Express* at me.

'But her victim was stabbed to death on a moving train.'

'Yeah but they got away with it, 'cos no one could prove who administered the fatal blow. I mean what can they do, lock up the entire village?'

'Er well actually ... ' I looked around and everyone was giving me the look, the identical look that you'd give Fat Clarry when he declared 'everybody out' and you still hadn't had your go on the pool table even though you'd already paid.

I swallowed a trifle nervously but continued anyway, because I knew that unfortunately for the majority of people, real life was never anything like it was portrayed to be in a book.

' ... look they would, okay, they would lock everyone up because if they didn't there would be anarchy and a breakdown in law and order. Oh and another thing, what if the evil-minded old bastard has a gun on him and one of you gets killed?'

They looked uneasily around and several nodded reluctantly in agreement.

'He won't have a gun, and he won't have the chance to get up and run away,' Vinnie stated and such was his authority that we all believed him.

After that Vinnie went through his plan; his dad would go up and beg for his old job back. My uncle would probably give it to him because his present driver was at that very moment in the public bar telling all and sundry that he was going to quit the following day. Fat Clarry who had at that moment pushed a couple of drinks through the hatch in the wall nodded and confirmed that this was because there was not enough money in the world to pay anyone to look after the old scrote for more than a week and the driver in question was off back to the rigs where the pay was much better.

Vinnie nodded, took a sip of his drink and then continued with outlining his cunning plan.

'Then as soon my old man is told to take the car out he will ring me. I will ring everyone else and the old man will then drive Mr Moncreiff to the quarry by the simple expedient of locking all the doors and the plate glass bullet-proof divider. This would separate Percy's seat from that of his passenger in the back and would mean that he wouldn't be able to hear him ranting and lose his nerve because he would switch the intercom off as well. And to make doubly sure that my old man doesn't chicken out I will get in the front passenger seat outside the old lodge house so dad doesn't have to drive the old bastard on his own for too long anyway.'

There was a murmur of agreement from everyone, as they all remembered how law abiding Vinnie's dad usually was.

'Then we will force him out as soon as we reach the gravel pit and let you lot start using him as target practice. There – simple, eh?'

Well it was a plan even though there were more holes in it than a Swiss cheese. I looked around the room at all these people who had known me man, boy and woman and felt a warm fuzzy feeling coursing through my blood. I also knew that they didn't have a cat in hell's chance of making it work, you see I'd read my uncle's manuscript and I reckoned that he'd already bumped off enough people to get him into double figures. And he was a wily old goat, a wily and very intelligent one.

I stood up and made my way to the door smiling at everyone who had to move to let me through. At the doorway I turned and looked Vinnie straight in the eyes.

'Agatha eh? Well that was certainly one of her best. Good luck to you all, great plan and I'll be off tonight so that you can put it into practice.' I gave everyone one of my best most brilliant grins and then I turned on my heel and left them to it.

I was halfway down the road from the pub to my house when the car pulled up beside me.

'Get in,' ordered the driver.

I opened the passenger door, clambered in and we drove off into the night.

Twenty-Five

Uncle Edwin didn't say a word for the first five minutes of our drive and neither did I.

'So,' he finally said, breaking a silence you could have cut with a blunt knife. 'How did it go?'

'They are going to lure you down to the quarry and then stone you to death.'

'Stone me, eh?'

'With homemade catapults.'

'Ah, shades of David and Goliath, almost biblical don't you know.'

Uncle Edwin seemed almost pleased by the method of execution which said something about his mental processes.

'Why tell me Alex? Why not let them do it? After all there has never been any love or even affection between our two selves.'

'For the simple reason that they have no idea how the aftermath will tear them apart inside until they can't even look at each other. One by one the guilt will eat them up and once the bravado has worn off it will poison everything they touch, their relationships, their health, and the rest of their lives.'

'My, my, Alex how poetical. But then you always were a bit of a girl, no offence meant by the way.'

'None taken.'

'Of course I will have to sell the house, not go back.'

'It might be safer.'

I took a flask from my pocket and took the stopper out.

'What's that?' Uncle Edwin asked as the escaped fumes began to waft around the interior of the car.

'Twenty-year old Oban malt, why?'

'Any chance of a snifter?'

'What? But you're driving! And anyway, you don't drink!'

'So?'

'You'd lose your licence.' He chuckled at that and then I remembered that he didn't actually have a valid licence in the first place. Uncle watched my face and chuckled again.

'Exactly, now let me have some.'

I handed over the flask which he took a great big gulp from and then wiped his mouth on his sleeve.

'Good stuff.'

'Should be, the amount the buggers charge for it.'

'Malty, peaty and something else ... '

I shrugged and held my hand out for the flask's return. The pig looked at me with his little squinty eyes and then took another huge swallow before handing it back almost empty. I scowled at him and then shoved it deep in my pocket. We continued in silence.

'So Alex, when do you think you can publish it.'

I closed my eyes and took a deep breath.

'Six months from the day you sign my company back over to me.'

'That's fair enough I suppose but ... '

'Look if you think for one moment that I can have that turgid piece of dross, edited, proofread and copy set for the printers, to say nothing of getting a cover done and the marketing in place, before the six months is up then you should be doing it yourself.'

'All right, all right, keep your hair on.'

'At least I have some!'

'Petty Alex, very petty, remember our agreement. You get your company back and I get my book published.'

I glared at him and then stared out of the window.

'I could have gone to the Book Guild you know,' he muttered eventually.

'Be my guest.'

'But they wanted too much, so I thought, why not take that rather wonderful publishing house that young Alex runs, the one that wouldn't even look at my manuscript. I expect that Caroline sent it back – she never liked me, stuck up little bitch.'

I forbore to comment and he shot me a sideways glance.

'Look we made a bargain. I don't have to talk to you about it and it's only the one book.'

'For now.'

I sighed. 'What!'

'It's the first in a series of ten.'

'Bloody hell, even Rowling had the good sense to give it up at seven,' I bleated.

He laughed at that, a laugh that was neither pleasant nor particularly amused.

'You can drop me off at the Little Chef, the one on the corner of the roundabout coming up next.'

He nodded and began to indicate.

I sat in frigid silence until he pulled up into the car park and I took off my seat belt before getting out.

'Stop,' he said, 'I'm coming with you, I could do with a break from driving.'

'But ... '

'I'll have a coffee – black and one of those pancakes with apples or some sort of fruit, bit of ice-cream, you can pay.'

He got out, glared at me until I reluctantly did likewise and then we walked in together, found a table in the corner next to the toilets and sat down.

The waitress arrived, gave me an odd look and him an odder one and took our order. Then I remembered where I had seen her before and the look made a great deal of sense.

'Shit, shit, shitty, shit, and shit.' I muttered and banged my head on the table.

'Alex!' my Uncle whispered commandingly. 'Will you stop doing that!'

'What?' I mumbled from the table top where my head was resting.

'People are looking.'

'So bloody what, you know who that is don't you?'

'Who?'

'The fucking waitress!'

'Alex mind your language. What about her?'

'She's Jason's bint.'

'Jason, who the hell is Jason and what in God's name is a bint?'

'Jason, Albert's son ... Mrs Maria Coaltit's toy boy. She is Jason's girlfriend.'

'Oh.' He looked at her and then back at me. 'Does it matter?'

'No, not really,' I hissed my voice dripping with sarcasm. 'She'll go and get our order and while I'm drinking it and you're gorging on pancakes she'll be outside having a fag and telling the entire village via Jason and his old man, that I'm bigger than Judas.'

He tittered, then threw back his head and laughed, he was still laughing when his coffee came. He laughed even more when Jason's girlfriend banged both cups down on the table, glared at me from kohl-rimmed eyes and stalked off.

I waited and looked at my watch. Then I took out my mobile and looked at that.

'Any texts to Judas yet?' My uncle asked and then he frowned. 'That's funny.'

'What?'

'My hands feel sort of tingly?'

'Really?' I replied and looked out of the window at the evening shadows and headlights of passing cars.

'Alex.'

'What?'

'I can't feel my feet.'

I turned then and looked at him with concern.

'Come to think of it you do look a bit peaky.'

'I feel strange.'

'Come on, I'll help you to the bathroom, I'm in enough trouble with our friendly waitress without having you throwing up all over the table.' I picked up my peppermint tea, took a sip, fixed him with a wry smile and then stood up, went around to his side and helped him to walk towards the men's room; at the last moment I opened the toilet clearly marked disabled and pushed him inside. I stood against it as he moved uncertainly to the toilet by use of the hand bars and then I quietly locked the door behind me.

'I have something to confess,' I whispered as he slid slowly to the floor.

'Oh.'

'Caroline didn't turn down your manuscript, I did.'

He gave a little shudder and then looked at his hands again.

'It will never sell you know, not really original enough and the spelling is just plain awful. It'll cost a small fortune in editing. Mind you, mother always said you were crap at English, even with all your airs and graces about going up to Oxford.'

He tried valiantly to stand and then fell back onto the cold tiled floor.

'Ale ... '

'Funny thing is that mother said you'd got sent down after a while, there was some kind of scandal. Something to do with cheques? You know, writing something you shouldn't. Bit like forging a will. And all those witnesses suddenly having all those little accidents. Couldn't but think it was your reason to kill number two.'

'Al ... '

'But then I thought, what would have been number one? Could it have been my father? What about this for an idea ... just a little odd plot, a scenario of my own. What if you and he went down to the old quarry and you had a big row and he fell or you hit him and maybe, just maybe, you hit him too hard or his skull was abnormally thin and, well, it was after all just an accident.'

I watched his eyes and they watched me. 'You can nod you know. You do have that much left.'

And then I saw the look of puzzlement and I knew that I had him.

'My father, your reason number one.'

And he nodded, a little nod but it was enough to make me smile.

'I expect I'll find out about number three in time and I'm almost certain that mother was number four. Number four was the one I never quite managed.'

And then he tried to sit up, the penny as it were, was definitely dropping and from a great height.

'Still there is always number five, the best one. I can see why you left that one until last.'

And then I looked deep into his eyes and I smiled.

'Thing about publishing crime is that you have so many reference books to look at, all that material sitting there just waiting to be used. All those wonderful organic poisons. You know the best things about poisons, the good old-fashioned things that Livia loved and Lucrezia Borgia and whoever killed Alexander the Great? No? Well I'll tell you, they very seldom actually test for them and most of them mimic other things, and you know the other thing? They wear off, get used up by the body and are almost undetectable. Especially nowadays when no one is even looking for them.'

I paused. The eyes staring back at me were as round as saucers.

'There is one, fascinating poison, it paralyses the body bit by bit until the heart stops and for a while the head knows all about it. And I believe that there is quite a bit of pain, but by then the victim can't even scream. Such a horrible and agonizing way to go and almost perfect for my number five. Of course you have to introduce it into something, like say alcohol, something with a strong taste anyway, just like, say

... a twenty-year old malt. And then if you want it to really work and work a little bit quicker you add caffeine, hence my not swallowing in the car and my cup of peppermint tea which by the way was delicious.'

He glared at me and then I saw understanding dawn in his eyes followed by despair.

'Oh and in case you think that my life will be ruined because I deliberately killed you in cold blood and with malice aforethought, I really think that you ought to know that I'm now going to help you to raise your head over the toilet bowl. I only have to press you down into the water which I'm going to first block with your own scarf. Oh didn't I tell you? I asked Vinnie to get it for me. He knows, you see, what I intend to do. All that stuff at the pub was just a cover story, something to keep even you guessing. And it must have worked because here you are.' I walked over to him, dropped the scarf into the water and pulled the chain. Water flowed in and then because it couldn't go anywhere as fast as it was going in, flowed up and out.

'And now I'm going to push your head in and hold it there until you stop breathing. I have no idea how long it will take, do you?' He tried to move at that point and I knelt beside him to whisper my final words in his ear.

'Oh but Uncle darling you do know don't you? Because after you hit my father even if it was by accident, you held him under the water until he stopped breathing.'

At that he looked into my eyes and I could almost for a brief moment see something akin to sorrow pass within his eyes. Then it was gone, with a look of pure hate following close behind and filling the irises with darkness.

'One last thing, you aren't the first but I'd like to think of you as the last. My own personal number five. Thanks so much for the heads up as it were. Oh, and in case you are worried that I may drag the family name into the courts, I'm sure that after the police have found the trophies in your safe, the manuscript in your desk and the body still at the bottom of the quarry they may actually believe me when I say that I don't remember what happened. Perhaps they will accept that you had a heart attack after I confronted you about my parents and accidentally drowned?'

I could see in his eyes that faint flame of hope fading.

'And now, dearest Uncle, its showtime.'

And then I pushed his head down into the water until eventually he went limp and the bubbling stopped. Then I walked back to the door and sank down against it until Vinnie and the police turned up and broke it down.

Twenty-Six

Vinnie found the flask I'd stashed in the litter bin beside the entrance to the Little Chef and Jason's girlfriend, who turned out to be called Clarissa, swore blind when later questioned by the police that I had helped my uncle to the disabled toilet and then come out to talk to her, until we both heard odd noises and I went back in to see what was going on.

The police almost believed her and they almost believed me but they still carted me off to the cells at the same time as they removed my uncle's lifeless body on a stretcher.

Constable Macleod and Angela Wainwright were about to let me go pending further investigations when someone from the 'Big Station' turned up and didn't believe anyone. He it was who was convinced that I had had something to do with my uncle's 'accidental' drowning. Then they went through Uncle Edwin's house, discovered the safe and all its contents, the manuscript he'd hidden in his desk and a more than incriminating diary which stated on the last page how we had agreed to meet and the following damming words:

... and if Alex ever suspects that I caused the death of both of her parents she will in all likelihood terminate my existence with extreme prejudice.

After that I was cautioned whilst they filled in the custody forms, took away my clothes, cash and everything else I had on my person. I had to wear something horrible with a zip and got fed a bap filled with something which had died and not gone to heaven.

An hour later they came back and told me I was going to be in court for murder, which I freely and tearfully objected to. They were all very nice about it, even the solicitor who had been on call and gave me a hug.

While I was waiting for the trial Trudy came in and told me not to worry and that she still loved me more than ever.

Vinnie turned up and told me that he had destroyed the hipflask and had assisted in the finding of the safe, the ring and the will and that the police were busily exploring all avenues to track down the witnesses; we both grinned at that. As he was going I called him back and whispered. 'You know that it would never have worked?'

He looked at me sadly and whispered back. 'Yeah I know, that's why I paid my mate Jazz to bring his rifle.' We exchanged complicit smiles and then he was gone.

Albert came round to tell me that they had found a body wrapped up in carpet at the bottom of the quarry lake, so I had been right after all.

Caroline nipped in and let me know that the firm was up and running and then offered me a book deal.

'Well,' I thought to myself as the court date got nearer and nearer 'at least I'll have something to do.'

Twenty-Seven

I wore my best suit to court and it looked rather good as I had lost a fair amount of weight. I also managed to look very much like Joan of Orleans before they set light to her, something which went down extremely well in the local rag and, according to Caroline, did wonders for our sales figures.

The court was packed as the entire village and all of my staff were there to cheer me on.

My solicitor, a nice young chap who didn't look old enough to shave properly, talked about my blameless character and I managed to actually look as if I had one.

The police admitted quite brightly that if my uncle hadn't have died he would have been helping them with their enquiries and Constable Macleod winked at me as he sat down, something Justice Mortmont carefully noted down.

After a while it dawned on both counsel and myself that the judge didn't believe me but did believe the rather flimsy circumstantial evidence in front of him. He was also for some reason hell bent on sentencing me to as many years in prison as the judicial guidelines allowed. Briefly I wondered if I should just change my plea and get a lesser sentence if that was what was going to happen, but everyone voted against it and I sat in court ever more convinced that I was about to be made an example of. I had no idea why, until I remembered that the honourable judge had sent me a manuscript a few years previously and I had sent rather a rude letter back.

I was, I had to admit, well and truly stuffed. Such is the world of Karma.

The audience in the gallery booed when I was given fifteen years, and I had to be helped from the room.

'I'll appeal!' Trudy screamed from the gallery.

'That senile git on the bloody bench needs locking up not Alex,' Old Percy shouted, which caused a massive cheer and an order to clear the court from the senile git in question.

I left to cheers and whistles and was driven off in a black van with very small windows to start my sentence, the length of which was something not even I had bargained for.

Twenty-Eight

I had a room to myself and the use of my laptop upon which I started writing the book that Caroline said that she would publish as soon as I was out. Everyone was very kind, particularly the other inmates who came in one by one and read or had the book read to them. Most of them wanted to be in it, so I changed the villager's names and used theirs.

The only name I kept as it was, was good old Uncle Edwin, who did at last get what he wanted, which was to be famous although not I suspect in quite the way that he had originally intended.

I was there for nearly a year before they got my appeal heard and I was released. By then Vinnie had found out that the judge had sent me a manuscript and that I had rejected it and then he got the press involved.

Finally, upon the day of my release, I typed in the last word, dotted the last i and crossed the last t of my manuscript. I sat back and surveyed the thick wad of carefully typed pages, it was most definitely the best thing that I had ever written and so the year hadn't been a complete waste of time.

Trudy picked me up, or rather Caroline picked me up and Trudy sat in the back and grinned. I realised why when

I got in and couldn't hug her because she was six months pregnant. My mother had made me keep something from before the operation just in case and Trudy had with my permission used them. Oh all right, I had no idea, but as I had actually done all the things that I'd claimed to in my fictional account of the murders in Little Comfrey who was I to cast the first stone.

I was still in a bit of a whirl after finding out that I was to become a dad and a mum when we drove into the village, the bunting was all out, and everyone was standing in the drive waiting for me.

All in all it was a brilliant homecoming.

Twenty-Nine

The book took off straight away and hit the bestsellers list almost before it was out.

Guy Ritchie rang up a month afterwards saying he had Vinnie Jones interested in playing one of the parts and would I mind if Caroline Quentin played me? It was that or Patricia Hodge. I said yes to both and then went back to reconciling the bank statements.

All in all it wasn't a bad year and eventually I'll be able to catch a train without having palpitations. Guilt is a terrible thing and one thankfully I don't suffer with all that often. I guess it must after all be some glitch in the genes, something I will definitely have to look out for the moment Junior starts crawling to the cutlery drawer.

Linda Mann started off writing poetry and plays for young people when her own children were growing up, branching out into novels and skits for radio. She set up Priory Press in 2006 with her husband Timothy to self-publish her own books and now has over thirty writers beavering away in various garrets across the UK and Europe.

Linda is a keen performer and supporter of the written word and apart from the odd stint on local radio and treading the boards in various theatres around the Island, runs a performance group of fellow thespians and radio presenters called 'Voices'.